"Come on, Laura. I'm going to help you today."

Little Anna grabbed the reins and pulled Rascal in the direction of the barn.

Once again, Laura's heart was warmed by the sweet child. What a shame this little girl didn't have a mother.

Laura turned and saw Owen standing in the doorway, light filtering around him so that he was merely a shadow. How she longed to run to him and thank him for giving her one more piece of her dignity back. But to him, teaching her to ride was just one more practical part of life on the ranch. Just another part of his job.

"Thank you again for letting me ride Rascal. I truly enjoyed it," Laura said.

Owen gave a jerky nod. "I'm glad. It's a skill everyone should have, and it's good you're finally learning."

His words confirmed Laura's previous thoughts. No matter how close she felt to him, or how much she wished for them to be friends, he was just doing his job.

Danica Favorite loves the adventure of living a creative life. She loves to explore the depths of human nature and follow people on the journey to happily-ever-after. Though the journey is often bumpy, those bumps refine imperfect characters as they live the life God created them for. Oops, that just spoiled the ending of Danica's stories. Then again, getting there is all the fun. Find her at danicafavorite.com.

Books by Danica Favorite

Love Inspired Historical

Rocky Mountain Dreams
The Lawman's Redemption
Shotgun Marriage
The Nanny's Little Matchmakers
For the Sake of the Children
An Unlikely Mother
Mistletoe Mommy
Honor-Bound Lawman

DANICA FAVORITE

Honor-Bound Lawman

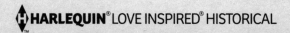

Recycling programs
for this product may
not exist in your area.

LOVE INSPIRED BOOKS

ISBN-13: 978-1-335-36956-7

Honor-Bound Lawman

www.Harlequin.com

Printed in U.S.A.

Trust in the Lord with all thine heart; and lean not unto thine own understanding. In all thy ways acknowledge Him, and He shall direct thy paths.
—*Proverbs* 3:5–6

To Princess and the roosters she's loved:
Mat, Myron, Tristan and Char.

Thank you for the inspiration behind Henry the
rooster. All rooster events in this story are based
on real events, and while they were exasperating at
the time, they're kind of funny now. Here's to the
challenges of having an accidental rooster.

And to Cowgirl: thank you for all your
horse knowledge and making sure my horse details
are right. I guess all these years of taking you
to the arena and watching you ride through
freezing winters, scorching summers
and all the days in between have paid off.

Chapter One

Leadville, Colorado
1884

Owen Hamilton shielded his eyes against the sun as he tried to make out the rider coming toward him. His small ranch outside of Leadville, Colorado, was too far from town to get many visitors.

His sister, Lena, stepped out of the house. "Were you expecting company?"

"No. Get inside and bar the door. Keep the girls close. You know what to do."

Lena hesitated. "Should I get your shotgun?"

"I've got my belt," Owen said, patting his hip. "No sense in drawing trouble if there is none."

They'd had this conversation enough times that Lena gave a nod. "We'll be inside. I'll wait for the signal."

Owen walked off the porch and headed down the path toward the oncoming horse. Now that the rider was closer, Owen recognized him.

He called over his shoulder at the house. "It's just Will. Put on some coffee and see what you can round up for refreshment. I'm sure he's tired after his long ride."

Though he sounded cheerful, his stomach filled with dread. The only reason Will would come to see Owen unannounced was if it was about a case. When Owen had turned in his badge several months ago, he'd made it clear he wasn't available to help his friend. Both Will and the sheriff had tried talking him into at least remaining a consultant. But after Owen's last mistake, he couldn't bring himself to potentially endanger anyone else. True, on that last case, no one had died. But Owen had gotten distracted, and because of it, a woman and her children nearly died. Though everything turned out all right in the end, he still couldn't forget how easily things could have gone bad.

As Will dismounted, Owen walked over to greet him. "Go ahead and put your horse by the barn. There's plenty of hay, and I'll get some water for him."

"Thanks," Will said, sounding out of breath. He must have been riding hard. And from the horse's sweaty flanks, Owen could tell that his initial instinct that this wasn't a social call was correct.

"Lena is fixing some refreshments. Then you can be on your way."

"You haven't even heard what I have to say."

"I figure I already know what you've got to say. When I turned in my badge, it was for good."

Before Will could respond, Owen's six-year-old twin daughters, Anna and Emma, came running out the door. "Uncle Will!"

"Pipsqueaks!" Will gathered the girls in his arms and gave them a big hug. Though Owen had no regrets in moving out to the ranch, sometimes he thought about how isolated they were out here. Living in Leadville, Owen's children had the chance to socialize with a number of families, including Will's. Though Will wasn't their real uncle, their families were close enough that it felt like it at times. Leaving behind their social connections had been a small price to pay for his privacy. If he wasn't living in town, no one could ask him to help on a case.

Maybe it sounded selfish, but Owen knew that if his fellow lawmen could just run down the street to ask for his help, keeping his badge hung up would be near impossible. Besides, he and Lena had grown up here. Lena hated the city, and they'd both agreed that they wanted the same kind of childhood for Owen's daughters that they'd had.

Lena had given up so much for Owen, quitting her job as a teacher to move in with him and help take care of his daughters when his late wife left him nearly six years ago. It seemed only fair that Owen look toward Lena's comfort. Lena had no intention of ever marrying, and after Owen's disastrous marriage, he wasn't too interested in finding a wife either. Which made being out here, several miles from town, perfect for both of them.

But as Owen watched Will laughing with his

daughters, he couldn't help but wonder if the best thing for him and Lena was not the best thing for his girls. Even though they had each other, the twins missed their friends in Leadville.

"Are you going to spend the night?" Emma asked.

"Why didn't you bring Mary and Rosabelle?" Anna added. The girls loved spending time with Will's wife, Mary, and doting on baby Rosabelle.

Will laughed and gave the girls another squeeze. "I'm afraid I'm here on business. I can't stay long because I need to get back. But hopefully, you can come to town soon and stay with us."

"Then you'd best come in and have some coffee, so you can be on your way." Owen gave his friend a firm look. "Any business you have for me is no business I want. I told you, I've put that life behind me."

"You haven't even heard what I have to say."

Will's stubborn expression matched Owen's. They'd been friends long enough that they could spend hours staring each other down in this manner. They'd done so often enough in the past, with each of them having their share of wins and losses. But this time, Owen wasn't going to lose.

"Don't need to. I won't turn a friend away without refreshment, but you might as well get back on that horse and go home. Nothing you have to say is of interest to me."

Lena stepped out of the farmhouse, wiping her hands on her apron. "Now, Owen, that's no way to treat a friend. After all he's done for us, you at least need to hear him out. Will, nice to see you again."

Growing up, Owen used to tease Lena that being a schoolteacher was her destiny because of the way she always bossed everyone around. Even having quit her job, she was still good at giving orders. Lena was also his elder by a couple of years, which meant Owen got more than his share of Lena's commands.

"Good to see you, too, Lena. Mary sends her regards. Even though this is a quick trip on business, there are some cookies in my saddlebags that she insisted I bring."

"Cookies!" The girls spoke and jumped up and down in unison. "Please, Papa, may we go and get them?"

Owen sighed. Getting rid of Will wasn't going to be so easy. Not that Owen wanted to get rid of his friend because entertaining guests was always a pleasurable endeavor. But business, that was another story.

"Let's go get Will's horse settled in the barn. Then we can get the cookies and bring them in the house. It'll be a nice treat for all of us."

His daughters didn't need further encouragement. Laughing, they ran to the barn.

Owen looked at his friend. "I guess that settles that, then. Go tie up your horse, and I'll get a bucket of water."

Before Owen could head over to the water pump, Lena stopped him. "I don't know why you're being so prickly with him. You don't even know what he wants."

"Doesn't matter. He's wearing his badge, which

means it's official business. This isn't the first time he's tried to drag me in on another case. I can't do it anymore, Lena, I just can't."

His sister looked at him sympathetically. "I know it's hard. Don't you think he knows that, too? If anyone understands the difficulties you have with going back, it would be Will."

"Then why is he here?" Owen shook his head as he looked at the ground. "All these years Will has been telling everyone that I'm the finest lawman he knows. But I'm not. Will has more faith in me than he should. He's better off without me."

The crunch of boots on gravel made Owen turn. "I stand by my assessment of your abilities. That's why I'm here."

Owen stared at his friend. "You're wasting your time. Our friendship has blinded you to my faults."

"I wouldn't be here if it wasn't important."

Lena stepped in beside Owen. "That's what I was just telling Owen."

He'd been prepared to fight Will. But with Lena on Will's side, it seemed almost impossible to consider doing battle.

"Fine. What do you want?"

Will shoved his hands in his pockets and leaned back on his heels. His face squeezed tightly into an expression of a man bearing the worst kind of news. Owen had seen that expression on his friend's face often enough, probably too often, that had Will opened with this expression, Owen wouldn't have had to debate with himself. The words that were to come out of his mouth were irrelevant. No matter what they were, Owen would help his friend.

"James Booth has escaped from prison."

The words were as shocking as if Will had pulled the gun out of his belt and shot Owen.

"How can that be? They had him in maximum security."

Will's brow furrowed. "Apparently not maximum enough. Two guards are dead, and they aren't sure the third will last the night. When they catch him, he'll hang for sure."

"When did this happen?"

"A few hours ago. The prison sent a telegram right away. They think he's headed to Leadville."

Owen's heart sank to the pit of his stomach. This wasn't supposed to happen. He'd promised Laura Booth, James's ex-wife, that this wouldn't happen. Every day, when he'd escorted her to the courthouse for James's trial, Owen promised her that James would go to prison for the rest of his life and never bother Laura again. One more promise Owen had broken as a lawman.

"Does she know?"

Will nodded. "Laura's scared, but she thinks he'll head to Mexico, where he has connections, something he's always talked about doing. Laura believes that James will value his freedom more than anything else. She doesn't think he'll risk getting caught again."

Unfortunately, Owen knew better. The man thought he was invincible, which meant he wouldn't consider it a risk to come after Laura.

"Has she forgotten how many times he's threatened her? At the trial, at his sentencing and even when I went with her to give him divorce papers. The last time she saw him, he was like a madman, giving in graphic detail a list of all the horrible things he would do to her before he killed her in revenge for testifying against him."

When Owen had met Laura, she was terrified of her husband. James Booth was a womanizing charlatan, hurting everyone in his path who did not give him his way. He'd beaten Laura into submission, making her one more of his victims. But Owen, along with Will and several of their friends in Leadville, had convinced Laura to testify against James in a case where he had been accused of murdering his mistress. At the time, Laura had been hesitant to speak out against him. He had many friends and associates, and she feared that they would help him avoid the consequences of his actions.

Owen had been the one to convince her otherwise.

And now James had done the very thing Laura was afraid of. He'd gotten out of jail, and he was coming after her.

Will had been right to ask Owen to come out of retirement for this. He'd made a woman a promise—that he would keep her safe.

Hopefully, Owen would be able to keep that promise.

Laura Booth smoothed out the sheets on a recently vacated bed in the boardinghouse she owned, trying to eliminate every last wrinkle despite her shaking hands. A menial task, and folks often chastised her for taking on those jobs when someone else could easily do it for her. However, in the past year and a half since her husband—no, ex-husband—had gone to jail, Laura had found a new strength in life. Before James's downfall, she'd been helpless. A spoiled heiress who had servants for everything. And now she could do it all herself.

She ordinarily wasn't so jittery, but the sheriff had stopped by to let her know that James had escaped from prison this morning. The news wasn't entirely a surprise—she'd known that James had many associates, and though Laura's purse was now completely off-limits to James, they probably still felt a certain loyalty to him. Plus, who knows how much of her money he'd taken and stashed away before he'd gotten caught. Getting out of jail would be no problem for a man like James.

None of that mattered. She was fine. Everything would be fine. She had a new routine, a new life, and it would be fine. She just had to stop thinking about James and the potential threat he posed. And get her hands to stop shaking.

Though the sheriff had told Laura to be prepared because they thought James would be coming after her, she was trying not to worry. Many of his associates had gone to Mexico, and James would be safe from the law there. He wouldn't risk getting caught with freedom so close at hand. Surely he wasn't that stupid.

Yes. She was safe. Of course, she would be safe. She had no reason to worry, no matter what the sheriff said. He didn't know James the way she did. James was a coward, who would run rather than risk getting caught. Hopefully soon she would get her nerves to calm down. She wasn't the woman who jumped at her own shadow anymore.

Gathering the dirty sheets to take downstairs, Laura couldn't help but smile at how different her life was now. While everyone in Denver had thought Laura had the perfect life back then, it had been the most miserable existence she'd ever known. She'd had money and servants, yes, but she'd also been married to a man who'd only wanted her for access to the wealth and power of her family's fortune. When James didn't get his way, he abused her in so many ways that Laura had quickly learned that it was easiest just to give him whatever he wanted.

However during James's trial, when Laura was sequestered in a hotel where only the law could reach her, she'd been forced to do most things for herself. The more she did for herself, the more she found strength in knowing that she wasn't as helpless as James had always told her. She wasn't stupid, incompetent, worthless or any of the other horrible names James had called her.

One lawman in particular, Owen Hamilton, had given her the courage to do a lot of things for herself that she would have never imagined doing. Including divorcing James. Owen had even gone with her to present James with the divorce papers. A formality—however, it made Laura feel good to know that she could stand up to James once and for all.

Laura stood tall as she stepped back and examined her handiwork. The room was crisp, clean and beautiful.

After James's trial, Laura had moved from Denver to Leadville, where she had opened her own boardinghouse. It wasn't your usual sort of boardinghouse. Rather, it was meant for women like herself, women who were out of options and had no place to stay. It was so easy for men like James to catch up with their supposedly errant wives. The law was always on the husband's side. A fact Laura knew only too well, considering all the times she'd tried to escape James's clutches. Well, it hadn't been all that many times. She'd learned rather quickly that running did her no good. And so she'd lived her life in meek acceptance because anything else seemed far too frightening.

Laura moved to the next room to pick up the rumpled sheets from the bed she'd already changed. Fortunately the last two boarders had left under good circumstances. They'd gone to stay with relatives who could support and protect them.

For once, Laura's boardinghouse was empty. On one hand, she'd miss the company, but on the other hand, it was nice to have a break.

As Laura went down the steps, carrying the bundle of laundry, she saw someone on her front porch.

Owen Hamilton.

Funny that Laura had just been thinking about him, and here he was, standing on her doorstep. With sandy blond hair that hung in shaggy waves around his face and blue eyes that probably pierced even the most hardened criminal's heart, Owen was still as devastatingly handsome as ever. True, his hair was longer and more unkempt, and he'd grown an equally unkempt beard, with rugged clothes to match, but there was no mistaking those warm eyes. Most people wouldn't recognize him. Except for someone who'd grown to trust those eyes.

Even when Laura had been under his protection all those months ago, she'd felt a strange pull to him. There was something about Owen that drew her in a way she couldn't explain. However, Owen had always been extremely professional. And so Laura kept Owen in that special place in her heart where all those schoolgirl crushes resided. Something to be sighed over with friends, but never acted upon.

She'd exercised such poor judgment in marrying James, thinking he loved her when he'd only loved her money. Back when they were courting, she'd thought him different from all the other men of her acquaintance. His character seemed above reproach. Back then, she'd mistaken the little ways he'd tried to control her as concern or caring. Of course, it hadn't been until after they'd been married that he'd first hit her.

Entertaining romantic notions about anyone else… Laura couldn't fathom doing such a thing except in the secret places of her heart. Her judgment was too poor, and even if someone as honorable as Owen declared his undying love for her, could she believe it to be true?

Laura opened the door and smiled at him. "It's so nice to see you. What brings you here?"

Owen didn't smile back. Unfortunately, that lack of smile told Laura everything she needed to know.

"I already heard. The sheriff was here to see me."

"Good. Then we don't have to waste time on explanations and small talk."

"It's not as though you've ever made a social visit before." She sounded harsh, and she knew it, but after her short reminiscence about him, it stung to realize that he'd simply moved on with his life after the time they'd shared.

He took a step back as though she'd slapped him with the truth. In a way, it felt good to make him feel that way. After all, all those months in Denver, awaiting James's trial, and the connection Laura had thought they'd shared… But when Owen had moved from Denver to Leadville, he hadn't once come to visit her. She'd known he was in town, had even waved to him from across the church, but he hadn't come to call. Even with their mutual friends, Laura was surprised at how little their paths crossed. No one brought up Owen in conversation, and it wouldn't have been right for Laura to mention him either. It was as though their friendship in Denver had never happened.

Which was why Laura knew anything she felt for Owen was simply a schoolgirl infatuation. To Owen, Laura was just another case. Any thought she had that there might be something romantic was just a foolish notion, best put aside for someone who had more sense about the ways of women and men than she had.

"I suppose I should apologize for that," Owen said. He shifted his weight uneasily on the porch. "The truth is, I don't know what to say to you. I mean, we're not...supposed to...become friends...with the people we're hired to protect."

Laura's heart twisted, and her mouth opened to give a retort back, but then she realized he was only speaking the truth. Any implied gestures of friendship were just that—implied. Further proof that Laura couldn't trust herself when it came to her heart.

"You're right. I'm sorry. That was unkind of me." She softened her expression and started again. "Would you like to come in?"

Owen gave a quick nod. "I think that would be best."

There was a stiffness to Owen that hadn't been there before. He was more formal, like her comment about his job had wounded him or perhaps had just reminded him of the truth. She truly had thought they'd become friends. Laura and Owen had been able to talk for hours, and sometimes at night, when Laura could not sleep for fear of the nightmares overtaking her, Owen would open the door to the hallway outside her room and sit with her. He on the chair outside the door, and she on a chair inside, so that no one could question the propriety of his actions.

As Laura stared at the lines on his face, she noted that new ones had formed where previously there been smooth skin. What had happened to him in the past year or so? Then, with a pang, she realized that in all of their talks, it had mostly been about her. She didn't know anything about Owen Hamilton. Well, she knew that he liked his coffee strong and black. That when focused on a task, he seemed to be able to shut out everything else around him. He laughed at her jokes, which no one else seemed to understand. And he was kind, always thinking about her needs and putting himself out to make sure she had every comfort he could possibly provide. But anything else about him? Laura couldn't say.

Where was he from originally? How long had he been a lawman? Why had he become a lawman? She couldn't claim to know anything about his family or his hobbies outside of his work.

No wonder he considered her a job and not a friend. And no wonder Laura was so clueless when it came to matters of the heart. She would do better in the future to remember that any feelings she might be developing were based on her ignorance, not anything real.

Laura smiled at him and gestured toward the sofa in the parlor. "Please sit down. If you'll give me a moment, I can find some refreshments. It won't take long to make a pot of coffee."

Owen shook his head. "As you've already surmised, this isn't a social call. We need to get you somewhere safe."

"What do you mean, 'somewhere safe'?"

"James wants you dead. This is the first place he'll look."

Laura shook her head. "Maybe, but what he wants more than my death is his freedom. He can't have enjoyed all that time in prison. Some of his associates are already in Mexico. He'll go there."

Information she'd already given the sheriff, which is why it seemed strange to have Owen here. He should know this already.

Owen looked at her like she was still the helpless woman he'd once protected. "You underestimate him. You destroyed James's pride in the worst way. He's coming after you. A man as arrogant as James is going to think that he can come to town unnoticed, kill you, then go on his way."

Determination set in Laura. She wasn't that woman anymore. The woman James had married didn't exist anymore, much of that thanks to Owen. Besides, she knew James better than Owen did. "James isn't stupid. He's got to know that this is the first place the law will come looking."

At the core, that's the only thing that gave her hope that she'd be safe. James always took the easy way out, which was why he'd killed his mistress rather than have his infidelity exposed. But to kill someone he'd publicly threatened, who would surely be guarded…that was too complicated for a man like him.

Owen looked like he disagreed with Laura's assessment, like she had no clue what she was up against. She squared her shoulders and looked him in the eye.

"Even if he does come after me, I still remember all the things you taught me. I keep a gun in my nightstand drawer. And just like you showed me, every now and again, I go out and practice shooting it."

Owen continued staring at her like she was an ignorant child. "A gun gives a person a false sense of safety. Many a fool has gotten killed thinking a gun was all they needed to stay safe. James is coming after you, and that itty-bitty gun of yours isn't enough to save you."

"You're the one who gave me that gun!" Now she was starting to get offended. Why had he even bothered to teach her these things if he didn't think her capable of taking care of herself?

"Yes, ma'am, I did. And I'm glad I gave it to you. I have no doubt that it has given you a great deal of comfort, knowing that you have the ability to protect yourself. But you aren't protecting yourself against an ordinary villain, and you know it. James is the worst kind of villain, and he won't stop until he gets what he wants...or he's dead."

Though Owen's words had some logic to them, he'd forgotten that Laura had been married to James for nearly ten years. She of all people knew what he was capable of, and Owen still treated her like she knew nothing.

"But James doesn't know that I've moved to Leadville. He won't know where to find me. Even if he does, Leadville is in the complete opposite direction of where he'll be headed. He won't waste that much time in search of me."

Owen looked at her like she was an idiot. "You don't think he can read a newspaper? Even I've seen the ads for your boardinghouse. It's noble of you, making sure women know that they have a place to go when they're in danger from their husbands. But this house, it isn't safe. Any determined man can get in and hurt the people inside."

He looked around the room as if to take in the surroundings and judge them. She tried to see it through his eyes. The pretty glass vase full of flowers could easily be used as a weapon. The windows, while locked shut, could be broken and someone could come in. As much as Laura hated to admit it, Owen was right. Not just about James, but about the fact that all this time she'd given herself a false sense of security.

"So what now?" Laura sighed as she sat in her favorite chair. How had she gone from feeling strong to being so helpless in so short a time?

"You'll come with me. I'll take you somewhere safe, where James can't find you. You'll stay there until the authorities capture him and put him back in prison."

"How long will that take?" Just because she felt helpless didn't mean she had to act that way. Or let Owen make decisions without giving her all the information.

"I don't know. My hope is that they get him before he ever arrives in Leadville. But so far, all we have is dead bodies to let us know where he's been, and where we think he's going."

Which sounded an awful lot like Owen was trying to get her to act on her fear of James when Laura had moved beyond that phase of her life. She wasn't going to live in fear of what James might do.

"So he's not here yet?"

"Not yet. But he's coming."

Laura took a deep breath. "Where are we going?"

"Somewhere safe. You'll know when we get there."

More lack of information and the expectation that Laura was the helpless woman she'd once been. However, these days, she had more to worry about than just her own comfort. "But what about my boarding-house? The women who stay here need me."

Owen looked around the room again. "Doesn't look like you have any boarders right now."

"Not right now, but I'm expecting some soon."

"They've made reservations?"

Laura hated the way he pried into her business like he knew it. But as she looked into those deep blue, knowing eyes, she saw that it was futile to argue. He was the law. He probably already had all that information.

"All right, I'm not expecting anyone in particular. But you know how these things work. My house is empty one day, and the next day it is full of people needing a place to stay. I can't just leave. What if someone needs me?"

She stood and crossed her arms, glaring at him. He had to see that she'd changed. That she could take care of herself if need be.

"You can't help someone if you're dead."

A good point and Owen's satisfied expression told her that he knew it. He always knew these things, and it seemed useless to argue. Except…she couldn't just leave.

Somehow running away felt a lot like giving up the hard-won strength she'd developed since being on her own.

"Can't you stay here with me until we know he's been apprehended?"

Owen shook his head. "That's not possible. I have obligations that require me to be elsewhere."

His answer made something in Laura snap. It wasn't right that everyone else expected Laura to do the bending. Meek, biddable Laura. A woman who no longer existed.

And if Owen thought she was still that woman, well, maybe she wasn't the only one misjudging someone else.

"So this is actually about you and your obligations, not about keeping me safe."

Owen let out a long sigh like he'd finally gotten irritated with all of Laura's questions. Back when he'd protected her before, she'd easily acquiesced to everything he wanted. She'd easily acquiesced to everything in her life. She'd been the most agreeable person anyone knew. However, over the past several months, Laura had learned that she had an opinion on a lot of things. She didn't quickly agree to every suggestion people gave her. She didn't let people tell her what to do. Instead, she took the time to think about what she wanted. When she finally got out from under James's thumb and had been able to create a life for herself, Laura had decided that she wasn't going to ever again do anything she didn't want to do.

If Owen thought she was going to simply do what he wanted, well, that was too bad.

"I'm sorry to inconvenience you, but I believe I'll stay here."

"This isn't a negotiation," Owen said. "The only option you have is to come with me."

Chapter Two

Riding on a horse with Owen, leaving her board-inghouse, made Laura feel more like a coward than she ever had. She'd finally learned to stand up to James, and here she was, running from him. Worse, she hadn't even felt like she'd had a choice but to go with Owen. How had she become so helpless again?

"You could have at least let me say goodbye to my friends," she said, not bothering to hide the anger in her voice. "And what about my boardinghouse?"

Owen had only given her enough time to pack a bag. Even then, he'd stood above her, telling her what she could and couldn't bring. While the rational part of her reminded herself that he was a lawman who knew what he was doing, the woman who had made so many strides in becoming independent resented his interference.

Funny how just hours ago, she'd been entertaining the foolish thought that he might have had some per-sonal interest in her. Maybe she wasn't a good judge of character, but she at least knew the signs of a bully. She'd been married to the worst of them, so for Owen to be so forceful with her, perhaps it was just as well that he'd never given her any indication that their relationship was anything more than professional. She wouldn't risk getting her heart involved with a man who showed such obvious signs of needing to have power and be in control. At least that was one area where Laura could remain strong.

"I told you, Will has arranged for some of the ladies at church to help out with the boardinghouse."

"How would he have had time to do that already? James only escaped this morning."

"We agreed when he sent me to get you, that he would talk to his wife, Mary, and she would rally the ladies. I have no reason to doubt his word."

Owen made a sound with his mouth that Laura had never heard before. But his horse seemed to understand what it meant because it sped up.

Laura clung tighter to Owen's back, hating the impropriety of riding double with a man, but knowing it was the only option. Though it seemed inconceivable that a woman of her age couldn't ride a horse, she'd never had a reason to ride until now. She'd always had carriages, and her parents had thought riding too dangerous a pursuit for young ladies.

And at this speed, Laura could see why.

"Do we have to go so fast?"

This time, the noise Owen made before speaking was one Laura knew all too well. Let him be irritated. Hadn't he been irritating her?

"As a matter of fact, we do. I'm deliberately taking a convoluted route to our destination so that if anyone has been following us, or tries tracking us, they'll be lost for sure. However, we have a lot of ground to cover if we are going to make it there by dark."

It had been the most he had said to her in a while. She should have been grateful for the information, and in the past, it would have been enough. But now that Laura had taken control of her own life, it seemed foolish to blindly trust this man, even though she'd done so before.

"When are you going to tell me where we're going? You said at the house you couldn't tell me because you didn't want anyone who might be eavesdropping to overhear. We're in the middle of nowhere. Surely you can tell me now."

Owen made another annoyed noise. This seemed to be how their conversations had gone since he showed up on her doorstep. Him needing to be in control, and her no longer living a life where she was pushed around all the time.

"What happened to the woman who used to trust me?"

"She grew up. Learned to take charge of her own life. And now she resents the fact that you've swooped in, taken over and coerced her from her home and are making her go somewhere without revealing the destination."

Owen let out a long sigh. "I wouldn't have had to coerce, as you say, if you'd just listened to reason."

His condescending tone rattled something in her.

She didn't deserve to be spoken to like that. "Funny, James used to say the same thing."

The reminder killed any remnants of those schoolgirl dreams she might have once had of Owen. He wasn't the man she thought he was, and now that she knew she didn't need a man, she wasn't interested in one like him. How had she been so blind?

He pulled back on the reins and asked the horse to stop. Owen got off the horse, then helped Laura to the ground, giving her a glare.

"Fine. Have it your way." Owen pointed in the direction from which they'd come. "Town's that way. I promised I'd protect you and that I would never let James hurt you again. But it seems to me that you are determined to let that man kill you. And now you want to compare me to him? Fine. I can act like James. He'd have no problem letting a woman fend for herself in the middle of nowhere. You want to be free so bad? Have at it."

He turned on his heel and walked over to his saddlebags, where he untied the canteen, then took a long drink out of it. When he finished, he walked to the front of the horse, poured a bit of water into his hands, and stuck it under the horse's mouth so he could drink.

Owen appeared to be completely oblivious to Laura. She looked in the direction he'd indicated, remembering how long it had taken them to get this far. On foot, there was no way she'd get back to town by nightfall. Even if James wasn't potentially out there, the danger she faced as a woman alone made such a choice impossible.

"I just don't know why you can't tell me where we're going."

"And I don't know why you have to argue with me about every little thing when I'm trying to save your life."

His tone hurt. Even more so, the thought that he would abandon her in the middle of nowhere. Was this the man she'd once had a slight tendre for? "Would you really let me leave?"

Owen held the canteen out to her. "If you have to ask that question, then I guess you don't know me as well as you think you do. I made you a promise, and I intend to keep it."

She stared at him for a moment before taking the canteen. Owen kicked at the dirt, making another irritated noise. "Sorry, threatening to leave you wasn't the brightest idea. I let my frustration get the best of me. I just thought that after all the time we spent together, you'd know what kind of man I am. I need you to trust me enough to go when I tell you to go and not spend so much time arguing with me about it."

Knowing it was a burst of temper didn't make Laura feel any better, even if he had apologized for it. He was so different from the kind man who'd cared for her in her time of need. How could she have not seen this side of him before?

Letting out a long sigh, Owen took off his hat and mopped his sweaty brow. "No, I wouldn't leave you here. I'm just extremely frustrated, and I don't know what to do about it."

"You could try talking to me and explaining what's going on."

"I never had to before. We had to get out of there fast." Owen looked back in the direction of town. "I just hope we got out fast enough."

More things he hadn't explained. "We've been riding for at least an hour now. Plenty of time to tell me what's going on."

"Possibly," Owen said. "But I've been busy thinking about what we're going to do. Figuring out the best route to get you to our destination so that any trackers who try to come after us won't be able to find us."

He went over to his saddlebags and pulled out some cloths. Laura watched as he tied the cloths around the horse's hooves one by one.

"What are you doing?"

"Now that we've gone a ways out of town and taken a break, I'm making sure that from this point on it will be even more difficult to track us. They might be able to track us here, and ascertain that we took a few moments to rest, but they won't be able to figure out where we've gone after this."

He turned to look at her and grinned. "I was once known as a very good tracker. One of the best. I'm pretty confident we can evade anyone who might be following us."

"You think James would hire a tracker?" Laura looked in the direction they'd just come from, staring out at the vast expanse of brush rock and a few scraggly trees. Most of the good trees had been cut down for wood—either to be used in the mines or to build houses. Some of it probably had been claimed for firewood. But as Laura looked around the area, it seemed as though she and Owen were the only two people for miles.

"I wouldn't put it past him. That's why all the secrecy. As far as anyone knows, I am no longer a lawman. In fact, when Will goes back to the sheriff's office, he's going to tell everyone that I wasn't willing to help him."

So many questions ran through Laura's head. She didn't even know where to begin. "Where will Will tell everyone I've gone?"

"He's going to tell a variety of stories, depending on who asks," Owen said, brushing off his hands. "He isn't sure who he can trust right now. James had to have had help from someone with a connection to the law. Though Will hates lying, we decided it would be best to use it as a means of figuring out who we can and can't trust."

Laura wasn't sure what to say. She'd always assumed that because a man was with the law, he was honest. Certainly, all of her dealings with Will and Owen, and the rest of the men they worked with, had all been very positive. But she could see where Owen's words might be true. After all, back in Denver, James had bribed many a man supposed to uphold the law. She wouldn't be surprised if that were what he was doing now. Though the trustees to her fortune had blocked James from accessing most of her money, James had still managed to steal a significant amount from her accounts. Not to mention the valuables he'd taken and sold. She didn't know how much money James had hidden away, but she knew he had means. Unfortunately, that put a lot more questions in Laura's mind.

"What kind of help would he have from the inside?"

Owen shrugged. "Could be any number of things. There's no way he could have escaped from prison without help. We just can't figure out who would've helped him, considering he killed two of the guards."

Laura's stomach knotted. It was one thing to know her ex-husband was a convicted murderer; it was another to know that he was still killing people. Especially since he'd threatened so many times to do the same to her. When she'd initially heard reports that he'd escaped, she hadn't been so worried because most of his threats to kill people had been nothing but bluster. His mistress was the first person he'd killed. But now, knowing he'd killed again, the way Owen was concerned about the situation and the extreme measures he'd been taking to protect her, she was starting to get scared.

But she wasn't sure she was ready to admit that to Owen.

"Feel free to walk a bit and stretch your legs. We've still got a long ways to go," Owen said, turning to tend his horse. He seemed to ignore her as he adjusted some straps on the saddle.

It was nice to walk, but it was also good to have some distance from Owen. Especially because the longer she had to think about the situation with James, and saw how Owen was acting, the more she realized that Owen was probably right. It wasn't like Owen to overreact, so for him to be this concerned…

But it felt almost like she was giving up all her hard-won strength to admit that she was afraid.

Being with this new version of Owen, it seemed like she was losing herself again to another man who didn't give a whit what was important to her. If it meant staying safe, he'd get her cooperation. But this time, he wouldn't get her heart.

"Drag your feet a little as you head back," Owen said.

Laura nodded and did as he asked her. It wasn't such a big deal to follow his instructions, and in hindsight, she probably had been a little too stubborn. But it was hard, after spending so many years doing everything everyone else pulled her to do without question, then finding a way to be strong and herself. Now, she questioned everything, and it was weird to fall back into that old pattern. Especially because it seemed only to corroborate Owen's belief that Laura was so easily moldable. Though his opinion shouldn't matter so much to her, what she wanted most was for him to see her as the strong woman she'd become. The strong woman he'd helped make her. Maybe it was foolish to care so much about what Owen thought, but she did.

Owen didn't look at her when she approached. "Let's get going. We've got a lot of ground to cover and not a lot of time to do it in. I did what I could to cover up our tracks and lay a false trail, and I'm hoping it's enough."

He was hiding something, Laura was sure of it. He might not be forthcoming with information such as where they were going, but she would find out all of the information about James and his escape. She might have been willing to let others take care of everything in the past, but not anymore. Laura Booth was in charge of her own future, and she would be a part of whatever it took to save her life.

Owen wished he had something better to share with Laura. However, his time protecting her before had told him that as much as she said she could handle information, she was too easily scared to do it well. It seemed like at every piece of negative information about James—what he was doing, what he was capable of and any time he threatened to kill her—Laura had turned into a cowering shell of a woman. She'd been afraid of her own shadow. Yes, he taught her how to shoot a gun. But did he trust that in a moment of danger, she would use it? Absolutely not.

He breathed in the scent of her. Fresh, like a spring day. It almost masked the smell of leather on sweaty horse. Riding on the same horse, with her behind him, Owen was almost too aware of her femininity. Laura Booth was a beautiful woman. Even now, riding hard to avoid detection, it was difficult to forget. But forget he must. Owen had a job to do, and he couldn't let a pretty face distract him.

"It seems as though we're riding closer to town," Laura said.

"We are, in a way. I wanted them to think we're headed in a different direction. But once we get to the river, we'll turn and head the right way."

"You're going to an awful lot of trouble."

Owen sighed. She just couldn't let it rest. "I told you—you're in real danger."

It had been a risk, going the way they'd gone and then backtracking, but the trail Owen had laid would keep pursuers from guessing his real intentions. As they drew near the cutoff that would take him to the river, Owen slowed Troy's pace.

"Now be quiet," he told her, lowering his voice. "Though it's not likely, we could potentially run into other people here. I don't want anyone to overhear us. Please, if you want to live, you've got to cooperate."

He could feel her bristle at his words. The trouble with being in such close quarters was that it was difficult to hide one's true emotions. Owen supposed that after all those years of being pushed around by James, and now knowing the freedom of making her own decisions, it was probably difficult to have to obey someone again. But the situation was different. According to their sources at the prison, James had told the guard who lived to give Laura the message that she was next.

But Owen couldn't bring himself to tell her that.

The graphic details of James's threat had made Owen sick to his stomach. Laura used to have nightmares about all the times James had threatened to kill her. She'd wake up screaming and thrashing so loud that it would take a long time to calm her. It seemed like Laura was finally getting settled in her new life, feeling comfortable and safe. How could Owen take that away from her?

True, it was James's doing, but somehow by telling Laura, it made Owen complicit in the damage.

They made their way through the area Owen feared might be occupied. He stayed among scraggly trees, particularly as they drew closer to the water. There was no sign of people, but that could be misleading because if someone who didn't want to be found had heard them coming, that person would be in hiding. Owen scanned the area, looking for signs that anyone had been here recently. He found none.

He brought the horse to a stop in a protected area that he'd often used in the past.

"We can rest here for a few minutes if you like," he told Laura, his voice thicker than he'd intended. "I need to make a few adjustments to the horse. The bushes over yonder are a good place for privacy."

Owen indicated a place his sister often used when they came through.

"I thought we were in a hurry. Why are we stopping again?"

The woman was going to be the death of him. Hadn't he just told her why they were stopping? It was going to feel like a very long time in hiding if Laura kept questioning everything he said and did. Hopefully, Will and his crew would apprehend James

soon. Much more of this and Owen might find himself going crazy.

"I've got some things I need to do. Part of the plan
to mislead the trackers."

He dismounted, then helped Laura off the horse.
Ignoring her still-questioning gaze, Owen began
removing the cloth he'd placed around his horse's
hooves. While he was working on the front hooves,
Owen used his knife to remove the excess metal
around the sides of the horseshoes. If anyone picked
up his tracks here, they would assume it was a different horse because the prints wouldn't match.

Yes, this was costing them precious time, at least
in the short run. But hopefully, it would send James
and his men on a wild goose chase, searching for
Laura in all the wrong places.

When Owen got to the back hooves, Laura knelt
beside him. "Can I help?"

Some of the irritation he'd been feeling washed
away. One of the things he'd liked about Laura was
that she always wanted to help. There were some
women he'd had to protect who expected him to
wait on them hand and foot. Not Laura. She'd done
what she could herself and asked him to teach her the
things she couldn't.

"Thanks, but I'm almost done. Go ahead and get
yourself a drink or take care of your needs. The water
here is clear and fresh."

Owen moved to the last hoof and finished the job.
He picked up the scrapings to leave no sign of his
handiwork. As he stood, he stretched, allowing some

of the stiffness to leave his bones. He'd been riding hard most of the day, and it would be another hour to his ranch. Usually, it wasn't such a hard ride. But he'd like to get Laura there and settled before it grew dark.

He led Troy to the river, allowing his horse to drink. The water here branched off into a small pool where animals could drink, and children could play. Owen smiled as he realized that it would soon be warm enough for the girls to splash in the water. This high up, the water was always bitter cold. But it never seemed to stop the children from playing in it.

Laura came out from behind the brush, holding a ragdoll. "Look what I found," she said, smiling. "This looks like the perfect place for a picnic. I can imagine some family stopping here. I wonder if there's a way to find out who the doll belongs to."

As she got closer, Owen recognized the doll.

"I believe that's Beatrice. She belongs to my daughter Anna, who lost it some time ago. Anna will be grateful that you found it."

Laura's eyes widened. "I didn't know you had a daughter."

"There's a lot you don't know about me," he said, taking the doll. "I have two daughters. Anna and Emma. They're twins. You'll meet them soon."

"Am I going to your home then?"

Owen took a deep breath. He hadn't yet told Laura where they were going. A fact he should have rectified long ago, but she'd been irritating him so much that he'd preferred to stay silent rather than snap at her as he'd been doing. It seemed like they'd been communicating poorly this whole time, and Owen had learned over the years that it was better to say nothing than to have to keep apologizing for saying the wrong thing.

"Yes. My ranch."

"If it's your ranch, won't James figure out that I'm there?"

"Only my closest friends know it's mine. Belonged to an uncle who recently passed away. People don't know we were related. It's the last place James will look for you."

Laura hesitated, and for a moment she looked like she was going to argue with him again.

"He's not going to find you there."

She nodded slowly, like she didn't quite believe him, but had finally figured out the futility of putting up a fuss.

"Why couldn't you have just told me that?"

"I told you why I couldn't. Besides, if anyone figures out where we're going, it doesn't just put you in danger, but my family, as well."

Laura gave him a haughty look, reminding him of their very different backgrounds. "Then I'm surprised you are even bothering to take me there at all."

"It's the safest place for you right now. I just told you James won't be able to figure out that you're there. But for the sake of my family, I have to be extra careful."

Laura gave a tiny nod, then asked in a quiet voice, "Why didn't you ever tell me you had children?"

She was hurt, he could tell, and nothing he said

would make it better. It shouldn't matter to him that he'd hurt her feelings, but for some strange reason, it did.

"In my line of work, only my closest friends know about my family. They didn't sign up for this business, and it's not fair to put their lives in jeopardy."

"Oh." She looked wounded, like he'd hurt her more deeply than just bruised feelings. She'd been acting like that a lot—like their relationship had been something more, something deeper. That was the trouble with being in close quarters with a victim. They often read more into the situation than it was. Which was why getting too close to a victim was dangerous. People mistook the emotions of the circumstances for something lasting and real. But once the danger passed, so, too, did the feelings, and that's when the real harm happened. Owen knew all about that firsthand.

Which was why he intentionally kept others at a distance. Especially someone attractive as Laura.

"It's hard for me to trust," Owen said, giving her a regretful look. "My family is everything to me, and I can't put them at risk. You don't know the kind of people who would hurt them if given a chance."

Owen turned away and brought his attention back to his horse, making sure everything was properly tightened. Yes, bringing Laura to his home was a risk, but they didn't have any other options. All of the men Will trusted had families in town. It'd be too easy to figure out that Laura was with them. With Owen out of the law business and out of sight, his ranch was the perfect place to hide Laura.

Will used to tell him that he was overprotective of his family. But after everything Owen had been through, he felt like he was entitled to be a little heavy-handed when it came to protecting them. Especially his girls.

"I don't want to put anyone out," Laura said, shifting awkwardly. "Your wife won't mind?"

One of the reasons Owen didn't like talking about his family. A brief explanation would only give him sympathy he didn't want or need. But the longer explanation was even worse.

"My wife is dead. My sister, Lena, lives with us and helps me with the girls. Having you come here was partially her idea."

Will had suggested it. In front of Lena. Who'd gotten extremely excited at the prospect of having another woman around for a while. With Lena on Will's side, Owen couldn't say no.

"I'll try not to be a bother. Please tell Lena that I'm happy to help with any chores. I don't want to inconvenience her."

Owen grinned. "I wouldn't worry about Lena. You'll get along just fine."

Being around Lena might be good for Laura. His sister was the finest woman he knew. Not that there was anything wrong with Laura, but she could draw on Lena's strength as she went through this situation with James. Waiting for a trial had been hard enough on Laura, but waiting for a madman to come after her would be worse.

As Owen scanned the area around them, he felt confident that they hadn't been followed and that no one was around. But that could change at any time.

"We'd best be on our way," he told Laura. "We've still got a lot of ground to cover before we reach safety."

He helped her onto the horse; then he tucked Beatrice into his saddlebag. The girls had been mad he'd gone into town without them, but this would ease their disappointment.

However, judging from the still-put-out expression on Laura's face, dealing with her frustrations over the situation was going to be a lot more difficult.

Chapter Three

Why hadn't Owen told her about his family? Even though his explanation about not sharing his family matters in work situations made sense, Laura would have liked to think that their friendship had meant something to him. But, as she'd seen throughout the day, that friendship had only been an illusion. She'd thought of him as a friend; he'd seen her as a case.

How was she ever supposed to trust her feelings about people when she hadn't been able to get that right?

They approached a sign announcing Fairweather Ranch, hay and livestock for sale, Robert C. Dean, owner.

"Is Robert C. Dean your uncle?" Laura asked when they slowed up.

"Was."

With Owen so near, Laura could feel his long sigh.

"I'm sorry for your loss," she said.

Owen didn't respond as a house and barn came

into view. The occupants of the house must have been watching out the window because the door flew open and two little girls, with hair matching Owen's but in long braids, came running out.

"Papa!"

The tension in Owen's body eased, such a dramatic physical change that Laura nearly lost her balance.

"Steady," he said, a gentler tone in his voice. "Let's not have you falling off with only a few yards to go."

Laura almost made a comment about it being the change in him that would have made her fall, but with his obvious happiness, it seemed wrong to spoil things.

They stopped near the barn, and Owen got off his horse. His feet had barely hit the ground when the two girls wrapped their arms around him.

"You kept your promise," the girl in the green dress said.

The other girl, wearing blue, looked exactly like her sister, and without the different dresses, Laura wasn't sure she'd be able to tell them apart.

"I always keep my promises." Owen bent and kissed his daughter on top of the head, then kissed the other one.

Though Laura had always known Owen had a tender side, seeing him greet his girls, and the obvious affection among them, made her realize that there was a great deal of depth to him she hadn't known. True, she hadn't known many facts about him, something she was becoming more and more ashamed of, but she'd been so certain of his character.

The harsh way he'd dealt with her earlier today had surprised her. It had seemed so unlike the man she thought she knew. She also hadn't expected him to be such a doting father. All of her confidence about what a good man he'd been seemed based on her imaginings, not the reality of who he was. Once again, Laura wasn't sure how to decipher the man.

Who was Owen Hamilton?

And would she even know it was the real him?

"All right, girls," he said, laughing. "Let's get Mrs. Booth off the horse, so you can properly meet her."

His formality was just one more unexpected twist to the man she'd thought she'd known.

When her feet were touching the ground, Laura said, "Please, call me Laura. I don't want to stand on ceremony here."

The girls smiled at her shyly, hiding behind their father.

"Girls, please introduce yourselves."

The one dressed in blue stepped out from behind Owen. "I'm Anna."

"And I'm Emma," the girl dressed in green said. "We're very pleased to have you here."

Laura gave the girls a friendly smile. They were miniature versions of their father, only in feminine form. She could almost see Owen as a child in them. Though she'd always considered the fact that her and James's not having children had been a blessing in disguise, something about seeing Owen with his daughters created a longing in Laura that she hadn't expected.

She would never have children of her own, a fact she'd thought she'd accepted, but somehow, these children reminded her of her lost dream. Hopefully, she wouldn't have to spend too much time with them while she was here at the ranch. She was hoping she wouldn't have to spend much time here at all. She needed to get back to her boardinghouse. But also, having realized how little she knew about Owen had made her come to see that she was a poor judge of character indeed. People wondered how Laura could have trusted a man like James. She'd thought that her poor judgment had been a onetime mistake. However, Laura was starting to wonder if perhaps she trusted too easily and saw things in people too readily where perhaps she should be more cautious. She'd read too much into Owen's care for her. And now she felt like a fool.

Owen had turned to the girls and was giving them the doll Laura had found. Her heart ached at the sight, and Laura started to turn away.

A woman came around the other side of the horse and smiled at her. Had Laura not been aware that Owen had a sister, she still would have immediately known that they were related. Lena and Owen had the same sandy shade of blond hair and the same warm blue eyes that made a person want to believe in them. But Laura didn't know who to trust anymore. Though she still believed that Owen was credible when it came to upholding the law, when it came to their personal relationship, she had to remember that to him it was just a job. A fact she would also keep in mind when it came to Lena.

"Welcome. I'm Lena. You must be Laura. I've heard so many wonderful things about you. We're very glad to have you."

Lena's friendly smile made Laura feel like she'd known her for years. Of course, Laura had felt the same way about Owen.

"Thank you. It's so kind if you to have me." Laura returned the greeting with an equally friendly expression. "Owen says I'm not putting anyone out, but please let me know if I'm inconveniencing you in any way. I'm also happy to help with any chores you might have. I like to pull my own weight."

The girls ran off with their doll, and Owen joined them. The look Lena gave Owen appeared to be one of doubt. She wondered what Owen had told his sister about her. Did Lena think of Laura as the spoiled socialite she'd once been? Or had Owen been more generous in his descriptions of her?

"You're company," Lena said. "You just make yourself at home, and we'll take care of the rest."

Laura smiled pleasantly. "I insist on being helpful. It's the only way I could possibly feel at home."

Owen looked at her like she was being difficult again. She supposed that as much as he tried her patience, she probably tried his. Funny that they hadn't had such a battle of wills before. Perhaps it would convince Owen that Laura was a different woman now. It irritated her that she cared so much. Why should she care when Owen didn't?

"If that's what you want," Owen said. "As long as Lena doesn't mind. She's the real boss around here."

"Ha!" Lena glared at her brother. "Don't listen to a word he says. Owen never did anything anyone ever told him to do unless he already had it in his head to do it."

Owen grinned, a carefree expression Laura had never seen on him before. "I learned everything I know about being stubborn from you, big sis."

Watching the siblings tease each other in such a familiar way made Laura feel even more like an outsider.

"Don't you start," Lena said, shaking her head. "None of us have time for your nonsense. You've still got the evening chores to do, and I need to get Laura settled. Supper will be ready soon, so stop your yammering and get to it."

Owen gave Laura a look as if to say, *See what I mean?* then walked to the back of his horse, where he untied Laura's small bag from the saddlebags. As much as she'd resented Owen picking over her choices of articles of clothing that he felt were too nice, now that she knew she was staying on a working ranch, she felt a little better about his heavy-handedness.

"I'll just take this into the house for you," Owen said, sounding a little gruff.

Laura smiled at him. "I can do it. It's not that heavy, and Lena says you have work to do. I told you, I don't want to be an inconvenience."

He opened his mouth like he was going to say something, but Lena shot him a glare, and he closed it again. Laura would have to learn how she did that.

"That'll be just fine," Lena said, taking Laura by the arm. "You'll want to freshen up after your journey."

They paused so Laura could take her bag from Owen, and Lena led her into the cabin. The porch was wide and inviting, with a pair of rocking chairs and a porch swing that looked like the family spent many pleasant evenings sitting here. Inside the cabin, the space was larger than it first appeared.

With a formal parlor and dining room, the front of the house looked like it would fit in with any of the nicer homes in Leadville or Denver. Certainly, it had the feel of the home she'd grown up in. She hadn't expected Owen to be so domestic. One more piece to the puzzle.

"What a lovely home you have," Laura said, smiling as she took it in.

"Thank you. Our uncle built it for his wife, hoping that such a fine place would make her happy, being so far from the city. Plenty of room for entertaining guests."

It seemed there was far more to the story, but Lena turned abruptly and gestured to the stairs. "Your room is up here."

Apparently, being close lipped was a family trait. At the top of the landing was a wide window, giving Laura a clear view of Leadville across the flat valley between the mountain ranges surrounding the area.

"It's magnificent," she said, staring. "You don't realize what a beautiful city it is when you're there, do you?"

Lena made a noise. "Too much commotion, if you

ask me. All that noise, the smells and, oh, the mud. The city's much better from a distance. But I do agree that it's a nice view. Sometimes I like to sit here with my sewing. You're welcome to join me."

The first overture of friendliness from the Hamilton siblings since this ordeal began. Laura supposed it was just as much of a shock to them, having their lives upended so.

"Thank you. That would be lovely. I often sew with the women from church." Laura paused, wondering about this woman she knew nothing about, yet felt like she should have. How could she have known Owen all this time and not met his family? Not even heard references to them?

"I wonder why we haven't met socially before. I've seen Owen a few times in town at church, but you aren't familiar to me," she said.

A dark look crossed Lena's face. "Owen is very protective of his family. We only go to small, intimate gatherings where all the parties are already known to Owen."

She looked like she had more to say, but then she turned away.

"Your room is here." Lena opened the door nearest to them. "The girls are across the hall, and I'm next to them."

Stepping aside to let Laura pass, Lena pointed to another room. "That there's a bathing room. One of our uncle's attempts at pleasing his impossible bride. Has all the fancy gewgaws and gadgets rich folks pride themselves on. Let me know if you want a bath, and I'll show you how to work it. We only bathe once a week, but you're welcome to use it anytime."

Laura stifled a smile at Lena's disdain for the room. Or maybe it was the wealthy people Lena didn't like. In particular, this hard-to-please bride she'd mentioned. Laura'd had a bathing room in Denver, but it had seemed too much of an extravagance to install one in her boardinghouse in Leadville.

When Laura stepped into her bedroom, she found it to be well decorated and a very pleasant space. Someone had put a great deal of effort into the quilt on her bed, and a beautiful cross-stitch hung above it. Lena's work? Laura was almost afraid to ask more questions of her hostess. "This is wonderful, thank you. I'm sure I'll be quite comfortable here."

As she looked around, Laura realized that Lena hadn't mentioned where Owen slept. And that all of the rooms upstairs appeared to be taken. "But where is Owen's room? I haven't put him out of his bed, have I?"

That could account for Owen's sour mood toward her.

"Not at all. His room is downstairs, off the kitchen. Our uncle used it as a study, but Owen likes the location for making sure everyone is safe."

Laura nodded. That sounded like Owen. "He's very concerned with safety, isn't he?"

"He has a right to be," Lena said stiffly. "I'll leave you to unpack. The water in the pitcher is fresh."

Before Laura could respond, or even thank Lena for her hospitality, she was gone. Lena might have encouraged Owen to invite her to stay, but it seemed like Lena was just as closed off as her brother was when it came to answering Laura's questions. So many secrets, and even though Laura was curious about them, she wondered if she'd be better off not knowing.

She'd already developed feelings for Owen once, and clearly she'd been mistaken there. What heartache would she face if she learned all the things about him that he'd been keeping private, and he once again didn't return her regard?

Owen didn't turn around when he heard Lena enter the barn. "Hand me that liniment over there, will you? Troy's leg feels hot."

A few moments later, Lena handed him the jar. They had a good routine, and it was comforting to know he could always count on his sister.

"She seems nice," Lena said.

"They always seem nice." Owen rubbed the sore spot on Troy's leg. He shouldn't have pushed him hard that last mile. He'd seen signs that Troy was tiring, but he'd been so eager to get home. Owen just hoped he wouldn't regret that decision later, which he would if his horse went lame.

"She had a lot of questions."

"She is a woman." Owen looked up at Lena and grinned. "You should understand that better than me."

"You care for her, don't you?" Lena's probing expression made him turn away.

The trouble with Lena was that she knew him too well. He couldn't keep a secret from her if he tried.

"Of course I do. That's my problem. I care too much. About everyone. I can't care about the victims. You know the trouble it's gotten me into before."

Lena sighed. "I know, but you're a good lawman. A good man. You and Sadie were happy for a time."

He stood and looked at her, then recapped the liniment. "Were we? I don't remember. I was so busy trying to keep her alive, and she said she loved me, and I loved how that felt. Being the hero. Which is all it is with Laura. I know how she looks at me. A man would be a fool not to notice. But it's just misplaced gratitude toward the man who took her out of a bad situation and was the first man to be kind to her in a long time."

Finished with taking care of Troy, Owen looked around the barn to make sure he'd gotten everything else done.

"Maybe if you didn't push people away, they could get to know the real you and figure out if it's love or not." Lena gave him that stubborn look of hers. When they were kids, he'd have shoved her and then they'd have wrestled until someone yelled at them to cut it out.

But they were adults now, so he shook his head instead. "I thought we'd agreed we weren't going to do any matchmaking for one another. I have my reasons for not seeking out another wife, and you have yours for not finding a husband. So let's try to get through the next few days of having a single woman under our roof without your planning a wedding. Otherwise, I'll be forced to ask my various single male friends out for a visit to meet my charming sister."

"You wouldn't."

Owen grinned. "I would, and you know it."

The long sigh escaping Lena's lips told him that he'd won. Then she said, "I just think that you can't let your bad experiences keep you from a potentially wonderful future."

Owen picked up the saddle from where he'd hung it on the stall. "Great advice, sis. Let me know if it works when you follow it yourself."

He was needling her, but she'd started it. Some of their childish ways would never be broken.

"I just came to tell you that dinner's ready. Since we have a guest, I will be on my best behavior, and I expect you to be, as well."

Lena winked at him, and he grinned. His arrow had hit its mark, and even though Lena was aching to meddle in his love life, she wouldn't. Not now.

That was sometimes the trouble with being so close to his sister. It made it harder to be close to others who didn't understand that a man's best friend could be his sister. He and Lena had been through a lot together, been each other's rock when they'd had nothing else.

Among other problems in their relationship, Sadie had been jealous of Lena. To the point that Owen and Lena spent a good year without speaking. The hardest year of his life. And, it turned out, Lena's hardest, as well.

"I'll be there in a minute," Owen said. "Let me get this put away."

"Don't take too long or else I'll eat your dessert."

She stuck her tongue out at him as she left the barn, and he knew she was giving him his space before having to go in and deal with Laura. His first time protecting her had been so much easier when she wasn't questioning his every move and he could ignore the calf eyes she made at him. But now she acted as if he owed her something.

And maybe he did. He'd promised he'd keep her safe from James, which is what he'd been trying to do. But she was making it really difficult.

He put his tack away, then stepped out of the barn. The ranch was positioned so that they could see a rider coming for miles. On a night like tonight, with so much cloud cover and not much moon, a man would have to be crazy to ride out here with all the rocks and shrubs in the way. But James wasn't a sane man.

Still, as Owen scanned the area and could see the lights from town dotting the distance, he felt a sense of peace. James wouldn't be coming tonight.

When he went into the house, the family was already seated at the dining table, eating.

"I told you we weren't going to wait," Lena said before taking another bite.

"I didn't ask you to. I'll just go wash up."

He could feel Laura's eyes on him as he left the room. Not just her eyes, but the weight of those questions in her eyes. His appetite fled as he thought about having to sit at the table with her and make small talk about things he didn't want to discuss.

When he returned to the table, the girls had nearly finished, and the ladies appeared to be eating more slowly to give him time to catch up. Presumably to give him company so he wouldn't have to eat alone.

"Papa, did you know Miss Laura doesn't have any children?" Anna smiled at him like she had a whole day's worth of conversation to catch him up on. And she did, he supposed, since he'd been gone most of it.

"I do know that. And that's probably not a polite thing to say about a lady. It might hurt her feelings," he said gently.

Anna turned her attention to Laura. "Did it hurt your feelings that I asked if you had children? Papa says I ask a lot of questions that I shouldn't, but how do you know things if you don't ask?"

Owen closed his eyes for a moment and prayed for patience. Anna was an inquisitive little girl with a zest for life, and Owen didn't want to kill that spirit totally, but sometimes, she made it difficult.

Fortunately, Laura didn't seem to mind the impertinent little girl. She smiled at Anna. "It did not hurt my feelings. But thank you for being willing to consider them."

His daughter preened at being validated in her questioning of Laura. If there were ever someone with enough questions to match Laura's, it would have to be Anna. But Anna's questions were easier to answer.

Lena set her fork down on her plate with a clatter. Owen looked up at her, and she smiled sweetly. A little too sweetly.

"Girls, let's clear the table and let your father finish his supper. Miss Laura can keep him company. I'm sure they have much to discuss."

She gave him another sugary smile before picking up her plate and leaving the room. The girls followed suit, leaving Owen alone with Laura in the awkward silence.

"You have a very nice home," Laura said.

"Thank you. My uncle had it built for his bride."

"I know," Laura said. "Lena told me."

He gave a nod, then focused his attention back on the delicious roast Lena had prepared.

"I find it interesting," Laura continued, "that you both refer to her as his bride and not your aunt."

Owen set his fork down. Small talk was not something he enjoyed, nor was he capable of it. Especially because nothing about his life involved small talk.

"That's because we don't like talking about her. She hurt a lot of people, and my uncle stayed here, hoping that someday she'd come back to him. She never did. He put everything he had into this place, all for her. But she never appreciated it. He was never bitter, so I suppose we're bitter on his behalf. He was a good man, and he didn't deserve to be treated like that."

Something he and his uncle had in common. They both picked women they thought they could save, but in the end, they didn't have that kind of power.

"I suppose that makes sense, then," Laura said,

sounding a little too cheerful. She was probably hoping this would open him up to more of her questions.

"So the girls' mother is dead? I believe you said your wife died?"

Owen set his fork down and patted his lips with his napkin. "Yes. And that is all I will say on that matter. Please don't bring it up again. With me, my sister or my daughters."

He threw the napkin down on the table. "Now, if you'll excuse me, I'm going to—"

"You're not going anywhere," Lena said, reentering the room, carrying a pie. "The girls helped bake this, and we're all going to enjoy a nice family dessert and chat about things."

Had Lena heard Laura ask about Sadie? Her face was too innocent for him to be able to tell, but he had to think not. Though Lena liked to encourage him in that department, she'd never give a stranger such easy access to his pain.

"Owen, sit," Lena said. "You don't get to go off sulking tonight because your perfect little plans got ruined. We're going to have pie and get to know Laura better, and it's going to be fun."

Emma sidled up to him. "Please, Papa. Auntie said you might even tell us a story about life on the trail."

Owen shot Lena a quick glare. She knew he refused the girls little, and even though those stories were the last things he wanted to tell, especially in front of Laura, he would because the girls asked.

"Of course I will." He pressed a kiss to the top of his daughter's head, then he looked over at his sister.

"Even though Auntie knows I don't like to talk about those times, and she exaggerates about what a hero I am. But just as soon as I get this case wrapped up, we'll invite my old friend Harold out, and he can tell you about life on the range."

Two could play Lena's game of torment.

Ignoring him, Lena turned to Laura. "Don't believe a word he says about not being a hero. You can't imagine all the wonderful things Owen has done, the lives he's saved. He's the best lawman you'll ever meet."

The smile Laura gave him made the dinner he'd just eaten turn over in his stomach. Back to the hero worship he detested. That was the trouble with people thinking he was so wonderful. Owen wasn't that man. Just like Sadie had been all those years ago, Laura was over the moon about an illusion, not who he really was.

As a lawman, he'd made too many mistakes. Enough that he knew he didn't deserve to wear a badge. Maybe he'd even been too prideful in keeping his promise to protect Laura. Could he keep her safe?

Looking around the table at the shining eyes directed at him, he wondered if he should have brought her here at all.

Chapter Four

The next morning, when Laura went down to the kitchen, she found Lena already hard at work.

"Good morning," Laura said.

Lena smiled at her. "Good morning. Breakfast will be ready shortly. Owen is out feeding the animals."

"Is there anything I can help you with?"

Lena shook her head, then turned to the stove. "No, I have everything in hand, thank you."

It was the same conversation they'd had more than once since she arrived yesterday. She wanted to be useful, not a burden, in Owen's household.

"Please," Laura said. "Give me something to do. Otherwise, I'll go crazy."

Lena sighed as she turned back around. "Well, I suppose you—"

"Auntie! Tell Emma it's her turn to get the eggs."

"No. It's your turn. That mean old rooster got me yesterday." Emma held out her scratched arm.

"But I don't want him to get me." Anna's face

had the cutest little pout. It was hard for Laura not to laugh, considering how serious the two girls were taking the situation.

Lena sighed. "Well, I guess I know what's for supper then. Laura, come with me."

Laura followed her outside. "What are we doing?"

"Dealing with a mean rooster."

As they passed a shed, Lena grabbed an ax.

Laura stopped.

Supper. The mean rooster. The ax.

"You mean you're going to…" Laura couldn't even say it.

Lena stopped and looked at her. "I know you're supposed to be some wealthy heiress. But surely you know where supper comes from."

Laura nodded. She wasn't that sheltered.

"The way I figure, we take care of the ones who deserve it first."

Before they were able to take another step, the two little girls came running out of the house, crying.

"No! Please don't. It's my fault the rooster got me. I should have known not to get so close. Papa has warned me. But did I listen? No. You cannot kill him because of my mistake. Kill me instead."

Emma spoke with such passion; Laura had a hard time continuing, especially since she wasn't looking forward to assisting with catching tonight's supper. True, she did know that's where her suppers came from. But she had always hired help to do the distasteful task. Even at her boardinghouse Laura employed a young maid to come in and help with some of the household chores. Procuring the chicken for dinner was one such chore.

Laura closed her eyes and took a deep breath. Had anyone thought to look after Betsy? The young woman depended on her wages to help her family get by. At fourteen, the girl should be in school, but her parents needed her to work. Laura did her best to pay the girl a good wage, and when things were slow, she tried to help with some of Betsy's schooling. Maybe her family couldn't afford for her to go to school, but that didn't mean the girl wouldn't get an education.

But thoughts of Betsy's woes were the least of Laura's concern right now. The two girls had caught up with the women and were sobbing hysterically.

"Please don't kill him," Anna said. "I'll get the eggs every day, so Emma doesn't get hurt again. You just can't kill that rooster. He's one mighty fine rooster, and we should protect him."

"Yes, we should protect him," Emma tearfully agreed.

Owen came running up to them. "What's going on? Is everything all right? Why are the girls crying? And why do you have an ax, Lena?"

Lena let out a long sigh. "I was about to get our supper and dispatch the mean rooster that attacked one of our girls. But now these girls are saying they don't want the rooster to die."

Though Laura wasn't sure how well she could read Owen anymore, she could tell that he was torn between being exasperated with the situation and genuinely concerned for the girls.

He walked over to his daughters and knelt. "Girls, if that rooster is being mean to you and he hurts you, then we can't have him on our farm. It's just not right. We don't keep dangerous animals here."

The girls hugged each other; then Anna looked up at him. "Please, Papa. I've already promised I'll do Emma's chores. Well, at least the eggs part. She said she'd do something else for me, only I haven't quite figured out what it is."

Emma nodded enthusiastically. "And it was my fault anyway. Like I told Auntie, I was the one in the wrong. It wouldn't be fair to punish a poor old rooster for something I did."

Owen sighed. "I can't have you pleading for the life of every farm animal on the ranch. You girls know that we have to eat, and this is where our food comes from. So, unfortunately…"

"No!" The girls cried together.

"You wouldn't kill me if I was mean to my sister, would you?"

"And she's mean to me all the time." Emma lifted up the hem of her skirt to show a bruised leg. "See here? This is where she kicked me yesterday."

Owen's groan was definitely one of exasperation. But he wrapped his arms around his daughters and hugged them tight against him.

"All right. We'll give the rooster another chance. I'll go cut off the spurs on his legs, and we'll see what that does to keep him from attacking you. But if I hear any more grousing about the mean old rooster, he's going in the stew pot."

"Thank you, Papa," the girls said in unison.

Laura had never been around twins before, so it was interesting to her to see how they not only looked alike, but they seemed to sound alike.

As she watched Owen continue to embrace his daughters, something stirred in her heart. Back when he was protecting her the first time, she'd wondered what kind of man he'd be with a family. He'd seemed like the type who belonged with one. How little had she known. Watching him with the girls now, she knew she'd underestimated him, and that was saying a lot, considering that at the time she would have thought he'd hung the moon.

Maybe that was why things were so different this time around. Back then, she'd put Owen on a pedestal. She thought him everything heroic and wonderful a man could be. But when she realized that he was just doing his job, it had stung. All the feelings he'd stirred up in her were hers alone. So now, even as her heart fluttered at the sight of this man tenderly embracing his daughters, she knew that anything she might think he felt for her wasn't real.

Owen stood, then held his hands out to the girls. "All right, let's go see about that rooster. Lena, you can put away the ax. For now."

As soon as Owen was out of earshot, Lena shook her head and muttered, "The man has no sense when it comes to those girls. He would do just about anything for them. It's a shame their mother didn't feel that way, too."

Owen had said talking about the girls' mother was strictly off-limits. Hadn't Lena just opened the door?

"Owen doesn't speak of her. Just that she is dead."

Lena nodded. "There is not much about her worth

telling. I didn't like her the first time we met, and I never started. I don't know what Owen ever saw in her, except that she needed rescuing. In case you haven't noticed, Owen likes to do the rescuing. Today the rooster, tomorrow it will be some other creature the girls have picked up. He might be a tough lawman, but his heart is as soft as they come."

It was as if Lena's words were confirming what Laura had just told herself. Owen liked to rescue. And once more, he was rescuing Laura.

"He does seem to have a tender heart," Laura said, smiling at Lena. "I suppose that's why they picked him for this job."

Lena grinned. "That, and he's the best shot this side of the Mississippi. The other side, too, since most of them can't shoot worth the lead in their bullets."

Laura couldn't help but laugh at Lena's idealized description of her brother. It was clear that Lena adored him, and just as Owen had vowed to protect Laura, Laura was certain that Lena would do just about anything to protect Owen.

No, there was no hope for them romantically. Except in the few and far between daydreams she allowed herself to indulge in.

Laura and Lena returned to the house, where Lena finished breakfast preparations.

"I suppose if you want to help by setting the table, that would be fine. Usually, the girls do it, but since they're out there with their father, tending the rooster, you might as well do it."

On one hand, Laura was slightly offended at being

given a child's job. But at least she was allowed to do something.

They took the dishes out of the cupboard, and Laura set the table. When she finished, Lena was still busy in the kitchen, flipping pancakes. It wouldn't do to bother her again. Laura remembered that just outside the front door, there was a field sprinkled with wildflowers. She'd spied an empty vase in the dining room. Perhaps a little color at the table wouldn't go amiss.

When Laura went outside, she was once again captivated by the beauty of the ranch. She could see Leadville in the distance, so far away, yet standing strong against the backdrop of the mountains towering above it. Though she didn't have the same aversion to the city that Lena did, Laura had to admit that here the air was fresher and cleaner.

A quaint white picket fence surrounded the ranch house. Laura let herself out the gates and made the short trek to the field she'd spied from her bedroom window. Here wildflowers abounded, making Laura's own attempts at growing a few flowers around her house seem pathetic. As she picked flowers, she hummed one of the new tunes they learned in church.

In the vastness of the open range, Laura felt a sense of the bigness of God. He'd made all this beautiful land, and here she was, enjoying it.

She gathered flowers, continuing to hum the refrain. The only reason she stopped was the loud grumble her stomach gave. Satisfied at the variety of beautiful flowers she'd collected, Laura turned to go back to the ranch house. She hadn't realized she'd wandered so far. But just as she began to make her way toward the house, she noticed Owen storming toward her.

"Just what do you think you were doing, wandering off like that?"

His harsh tone made Laura want to cringe. Once again, he was speaking to her in a way she was no longer used to. Though she supposed she should start getting used to it. The old Owen never spoke to her like this, and it reminded her so much of James. Angry and accusing, without concern for her feelings.

"I was just gathering some flowers," she said firmly. When James would treat her like that, she would cower and apologize for herself.

But that was the old Laura. The new Laura had nothing to apologize for. She was her own woman, and she would not cower just because a man raised his voice at her.

One more reason to tamp down any affectionate feelings she might have for Owen.

"You can't just wander around here, especially without telling anyone where you're going. James and his men could be out there. Didn't Lena tell you to stay inside the fence?"

Laura tried to remember if Lena had said something, but she honestly wasn't sure. It seemed like there was so much new information she'd been given over the past day, that she didn't know.

"I…"

"I don't want to hear it." Owen grabbed her by the

elbow and turned her in the direction of the house. "You have to stay in the yard. If we were in town, you would be confined to being indoors only. Don't make me regret giving you even this little bit of freedom."

Laura jerked her arm out of Owen's grip. "And I don't need you manhandling me to get me to go back inside. I understand the danger. In the future, I will be more cautious. However, you don't need to be so rough with me. I'm not a child."

Owen glared at her. "Then stop acting like one. I'm trying to save your life, and all you seem to do is gripe about the inconvenience it is to you. At least my children know not to leave the yard without letting someone know where they're going."

"Is someone after them, too?"

He paused, looking like he needed a moment to gather his thoughts. Perhaps they both did, with the way they were arguing. Then Owen looked at her with a gentler gaze.

"No, no one is after them. But there are dangers aplenty out here. Though we don't get too many bears, they have been known to come onto ranch property. And then there are the mountain lions, who follow the herds of deer that like to graze in my pastures. When we were in town, you mentioned being able to take care of yourself with your pistol. Did you even remember to bring it on your little stroll?"

Laura's face heated at his words. She didn't have her gun, which was probably obvious to him since all she held in her hands was a bunch of wildflowers. As for his reminders about the wild animals, she did re-

member Lena warning her. She'd given a more exten-
sive list, but all the same, Laura should have known
better. Though Owen was still in the wrong for how
unkindly he spoke to her, she knew he was right. She
hadn't thought of the danger, only about brightening
the room with some pretty flowers.

"I'm sorry," Laura said. "You're right. I wasn't
thinking. I was enjoying the fresh air, and the idea
of having some fresh flowers in the house was too
tempting. I only thought to cheer the place up."

Even those words were wrong. Owen's face dark-
ened. "Is that a complaint about my house?"

Laura sighed as she shook her head. "No. The ac-
commodations are wonderful. I couldn't ask for better. But as you may have noticed from your brief visit
to my home, I simply adore having flowers."

Owen appeared mollified by her words. Not completely happy, but no longer as angry.

He held out his hand to her. "I'm sorry, too. I know
that it's difficult to be away from home and the things
you love. If I seem overbearing, it's only because I'm
doing everything I can to protect you. I won't let him
hurt you again."

The sincerity in his voice made her wish she hadn't
questioned him so harshly. Before, they'd gotten on
so well. But now, it seemed like they were constantly
rubbing each other the wrong way even though that
wasn't their intention.

Owen was just trying to do his job, not be her
friend. Besides, did she really want a friend with such
volatile reactions?

* * *

Owen followed Laura into the house, trying not to be frustrated. Once again, she had to turn everything into an argument. She'd acquiesced a little easier than normal, but still. Why couldn't she just trust him to keep her safe?

Worse, now he had to figure out what to do with an ornery rooster. When he'd tried to trim the spurs off the rooster's legs, the first one bled so much the girls thought he was going to die. Which had left his daughters in more tears. So he'd only gotten one of them off. He had put the creature in a feed sack and had brought it into the house for doctoring.

Which is when he'd discovered Laura was missing.

Now that Laura was accounted for, he could return to reassuring his daughters that Henry, which is what they decided to name the rooster, would be fine.

"Papa! Look at Henry. Auntie helped us bandage his leg." Anna's smile was a welcome ray of sunshine.

However, the rooster under her arm was not.

"What is that contraption on the back of him?"

Emma smiled at him. "One of my old bonnets. We put it there so's it would catch the droppings. Auntie said we could keep him in the house as long as he doesn't make too big of a mess. Well, we fixed that."

Behind him, Laura was trying to stifle a giggle. He would laugh himself, except he knew that it would hurt his daughters' feelings. More important, a rooster in the house was no laughing matter.

"What have I told you about keeping barn animals in the house?"

"But he's hurt," Anna said.

Emma nodded. "You let the sick ones in the kitchen before."

Owen tried not to groan. The only thing sick about that rooster was in his head. A few days and there would be a little scabby knob where the spur had been, making the rooster less of a threat. But he could still jump and attack with his feet. The claws were sharp, meant to fend off any intruders and to fight off the competition.

"He'll be fine. He doesn't belong in the house. As I told you, even missing a spur, he can be dangerous when threatened. The last thing we need is a rooster in the house attacking people."

The girls looked at each other like they were expecting his objection. Which was no surprise, considering the two of them often schemed together. Sometimes he was no match for twin girls.

"Well, Papa, we've been thinking," Anna said. "The reason he attacks is because he's scared of us. If we let him live with us for a little while and show him that there is nothing to be afraid of, he'll be nice."

Emma looked up at him with bright blue eyes that he was often powerless to resist. "Papa, we're going to train the rooster."

Train the rooster. Of all the harebrained ideas. But as Owen looked at his daughters, and the pleading expressions on their faces, he found he didn't have the heart to say no.

In all his days, Owen had never heard of a person

training a rooster. But if the girls wanted to try, he supposed there wouldn't be any harm in it.

"What does your aunt Lena say?"

Lena entered the parlor shaking her head. "It can't be worse than the skunk they wanted to train."

Owen let out a long sigh. Earlier in the year, the girls had found a baby skunk all on its own. Though Owen had tried to explain to them that his mother was probably out gathering food for him, and they should leave it alone, somehow their nonsense had gotten to him in such a way that he ended up letting them keep the thing in the barn. They were going to train that skunk not to spray anyone. Ha. Sometimes he thought he could still smell the remnants of that unfortunate experience.

"Have you thought about the kind of mess it's going to make in the house?" Owen looked at Lena, hoping she could tell from his expression that he was looking for any excuse to not have a rooster in the house.

Lena sighed. "So far the bonnet contraption is preventing any messes. And I will admit that, as of yet, the rooster hasn't gotten into anything he shouldn't. But I've told the girls that they are responsible for cleaning up after him, and the first cross word I get out of them about it, that rooster is going back into the henhouse."

At least this rooster experiment wouldn't last very long. Owen gave them an hour, maybe two, before that rooster created a ruckus big enough that Lena would banish the creature from the house.

"All right." Owen sighed. "If you want to, we can

try it. But the first I hear of that rooster causing any trouble, he's back in the pen with the others."

Anna and Emma exchanged glances. Then Anna gave him a stern look. "His name is not *rooster*. His name is Henry. If we are going to civilize him, then we must give him a civilized name."

A tiny giggle slipped out of Laura. Owen turned and gave her a sharp look. She obviously wasn't used to children, because anyone who was knew that you shouldn't laugh at their silly ideas.

"It's not funny," Anna said, giving Laura a haughty glare. "No one refers to you as *human* instead of your name, so why would we refer to Henry as *rooster*?"

Laura seemed to get the hint, and she smiled at his daughters. "Of course not. I was just thinking about how my father was named Henry, and they don't resemble one another at all. Except, of course, my father's nose was rather like a beak."

The girls giggled, and Laura giggled with them. Owen was pleased to see how readily Laura had joined in their game. She didn't treat them as silly, and she didn't openly mock their ideas. Some people thought the girls strange for the way they adopted every stray and injured animal they found. But Owen liked the compassion they were developing for all God's creatures. When they got older, their ability to gently tend animals would be very useful on the ranch. They could help with the doctoring and win the animals' trust in such a way as to make the work easier. Perhaps they could become veterinarians. Maybe that wasn't a traditional role for a woman, but nothing about Owen's family had ever been traditional.

The girls seemed to notice the flowers in Laura's hand, pointing to them and whispering to each other.

"I love flowers!" Emma, who was usually more timid around strangers, rushed over to Laura. "Next time you go pick wildflowers, you should invite us. It's the polite thing to do."

It was Owen's turn to bite back a chuckle. Lena had been working extra diligently with the girls on their manners, and obviously, this was one lesson that had stuck. And of course, it would. Those girls loved to traipse all over the countryside and would use any excuse to do so.

"But remember," Owen said. "No one is allowed to leave the yard without talking to your aunt or me."

The little girls glowered at his statements. Though they knew the rules, it was good to remind them from time to time.

"But all the good flowers are in the meadow." Anna crossed her arms over her chest as she stared at her father.

"And we can go to the meadow as a family at some point. But you and your sister may not go without either your aunt or me giving you permission."

The stubborn look didn't leave Anna's face.

"Laura is an adult. She could take us."

Owen hadn't explained to the girls exactly why Laura was there. He tried to keep them separated from his law work as much as possible. It was dangerous, and Anna already had an appetite for danger.

The last thing he needed was for his daughter to get it in her head that she was helping protect someone.

"Laura is new here. She doesn't know the ranch the way your aunt and I do. She's not familiar with the dangers, and wouldn't know how to handle it if she got into trouble. Besides that, she is our guest, not your nursery maid. So please don't bother her."

He looked over at Laura and gave her a small smile, hoping she understood that he wanted her to feel like a welcome guest, not an extra set of hands. Though sometimes they could use the help, he would do everything in his power not to inconvenience her more than he already had. He knew she was angry at him for forcing her to leave town, but this was the safest option.

She gave the tiniest of nods, but it almost seemed like he'd done something to offend her yet again. It didn't matter. Whatever bee she had in her bonnet now, she'd just have to get over it. Why she needed to be so difficult after being so cooperative the last time he protected her, he didn't know. And frankly, he didn't have the energy to find out. He turned his attention back to the girls.

"But you never take us to the meadow," Anna said. "You've been promising us a picnic for ages, but then you get busy, and we can't do it. Now that we have a guest, shouldn't we entertain her by taking her there?"

A picnic.

Owen shouldn't have been surprised by that demand; after all, the girls often wanted to go on picnics. It didn't seem like such a terrible request, and yet, Owen could think of dozens of reasons why it was a bad idea. The biggest one being the madman after Laura.

"We need to stick around the ranch." Owen tried to look regretful as he addressed his daughters. "We might have visitors, and I don't want to miss them."

Owen hesitated, trying not to give away the fact that he was concerned about everyone's safety. Here at the ranch, he could protect Laura and his family. But the farther they got away from the house and out onto open range, the more dangerous things were.

"But the meadow isn't very far." Those sweet little doe eyes Anna had never failed to twist his heart. When it came time for his daughter to be courted, he almost felt sorry for the poor unfortunate soul she decided she liked. Not just because his daughter was impossible to resist, but because Owen wasn't sure there was a man alive good enough for his little girls.

"I just don't think it's a good idea right now," he said, hoping it would get him off the hook.

Everyone, including Lena, glared at him.

Owen tried not to groan. Once his sister got involved with the girls' plans, saying no was as hard as sawing off his own arm. And probably more painful.

But it was the wistful look on Laura's face that got him. He knew she thought he was being unreasonable, and even though he had plenty of good reasons for all of his actions, he didn't like how she saw him as the enemy. She was just supposed to be a case. He wasn't supposed to care one way or another what she thought of him.

Yet something inside him yearned to have her look

at him in a different light. Like she had when she'd trusted him. He'd known she'd developed a tendre for him, and he'd done his best to ignore it. He'd gotten good at deflecting the misguided affections of victims he looked after.

The way she looked at him now, though, he'd do just about anything to erase the disappointment on her face. To make her care about him again.

Owen shook his head, trying to banish the thought from his mind. What was he thinking? Any feelings Laura might develop for him were based on the stress of the situation. Not real love. He'd learned that the hard way with Sadie. Once the thrill of being chased by bandits faded away and she was left sitting at home with a couple of squalling infants, she'd gotten bored of him. Of normal life.

People thought he was a lawman because he loved the excitement. Far from it. What he craved most was the peace he'd found here at the ranch with his daughters and sister. He'd only picked up his badge to honor a promise. But after that, once again, he'd be back to the quiet.

Falling in love with Owen the lawman wasn't falling in love with the real man. So to even consider… anything…with Laura—it wasn't fair to her or to him. He wasn't giving his heart to someone who didn't know the man behind the badge.

Still, as she continued to look more wounded than that silly rooster, he found himself saying, "All right. I'll see what I can arrange."

Chapter Five

After breakfast, Laura helped Lena clear the table and do the dishes. She was pleased that finally, there was no argument from the other woman as she helped out. Owen had been silent through most of the meal as the twins chattered about what they wanted to bring on the picnic the next day, then had gone to the barn immediately after.

The man was a mystery, and the woman standing next to her, drying dishes, seemed to be a clue to that mystery, only she wasn't talking either.

"Auntie! Look what we taught Henry to do. He just sits nicely in our arms now and doesn't put up a fuss."

Anna beamed as she held up the rooster.

Emma held out her arms. "It's my turn now."

Then Emma took the rooster and fed it a piece of bread. "See? He likes me."

Lena shook her head as she hung the dish towel over a chair. "Of course he likes you. You're feeding him. But what happens when you run out of the bread I was saving to go with lunch?"

"We'll do without. It's a small sacrifice to save our Henry." Anna stood tall, hands on her hips.

Laura was certain the little girl hadn't come up with such a bold statement on her own. Yet there was something so charming about how she'd adopted the words of an adult with the openheartedness of a child; Laura couldn't help but smile.

With that smile, though, came the ache that often arrived when spending time with other people's children. She loved children, especially these vivacious girls who defended a mean rooster. But once this time was over, she'd go back to her life, away from the girls, and back to the emptiness of being alone.

Not having children only bothered her when she caught a glimpse of what she'd never have. Some of the well-meaning women in church often told her that she could marry again and finally have children, but it was impossible. Even if she could trust another man enough to marry him, she still wouldn't have children. When James didn't get the heir he wanted, she'd visited the doctor—many doctors, in fact—only to be told it was unlikely she ever would bear children.

What man would want a woman under those circumstances?

It was always a risk, marrying someone and not knowing whether or not they could have children. But to know? Laura shook her head.

Lena turned to Laura. "I'm going to do lessons with the girls now. You're welcome to join us in the library if you need company. My uncle loved to read, and you'll find a wide selection of books to choose from. You may take one and enjoy it there, or find another cozy spot in the house to read. Or if there's another way you'd like to pass the time, you're welcome to do so."

Laura hesitated. These children weren't like her friends' children. At least in Leadville she could spend time with Nellie Jeffries and her children if the longing hit. Or she could even visit with Polly Taylor and her family. Or, if she thought about it, any number of women in church. But given Owen's guardedness, once Laura left, she'd probably never see his children again.

"If you'd prefer another activity, like sewing or knitting, I could find some supplies for you. I realize you wouldn't have had time to bring any of your own." Lena smiled at her, obviously trying to be a good hostess, oblivious to the true pain in Laura's heart.

Did Lena regret not marrying and having children? Or were her brother's children enough like her own that it didn't matter?

Laura took a deep breath. Dwelling on her impossible longing didn't make it easier. "Thank you. I would like to visit with Owen if that's all right?"

Why she chose to torment herself in another way, she didn't know. But suddenly, being in this place with two little girls squabbling good-naturedly over who got to hold the rooster during lessons seemed to be almost suffocating. Lena meant well, but she couldn't possibly understand.

"He's in the barn," Lena said, a resigned expression filling her face. "He won't like you bothering him, but I suspect you and I are enough alike that it won't stop you."

Her face softened. "Just be gentle with him. I can't imagine how difficult it would be to give up your independence the way you have. But this isn't easy on him either. He carries a lot of hurt, and having you here reminds him of it."

Before Laura could ask what Lena meant, the other woman turned away and directed the girls into the library for their lessons. Clearly Lena wasn't going to tell her anything else. That seemed to be the way of things in this household. Only giving small bits of information, and leaving the rest to wonder about.

Laura walked out to the barn, noting that while it was technically outside the fenced area of the house, it was still within easy distance. And Owen stood just outside the building. Surely he couldn't fault her for coming to see him.

"Everything all right?" he asked when she approached.

"Yes. I felt cooped up in the house, and I didn't want to be a bother while Lena did lessons with the girls, so I thought I'd come outside for a while. Perhaps we can discuss the plan."

Owen stared at her like she'd just spoken a foreign language. "The plan?"

Right. Because before Owen never told her the plan, and Laura never asked.

"To keep me safe," she said, staring right back at him. "That is why we've gone through all of this, isn't it?"

He didn't say anything but continued with his heavy gaze upon her.

"You said that I'm here until they capture James, but being so isolated, how will we know? They could have him in custody already."

Owen shook his head. "I've got a couple of vantage points from the ranch where I can see for miles. If any rider comes this way, I'll know. Will and I have a signal. There's been no signal."

Which told her absolutely nothing.

Laura opened her mouth to ask him for more details, but Owen shook his head.

"Don't push me. I've had all I can take for one day. With that rooster they insist on keeping as a pet, and now a picnic I have to plan, I just can't, Laura. Can you please let it go for now?"

Suddenly, he seemed tired and weary. Like the pain Lena had alluded to was catching up to him. And if James showed up, Owen would need every ounce of strength to fight him. With Owen being Laura's only hope at survival in this place, so far removed from civilization, she couldn't take the chance of having him at less than his best.

"All right," Laura said. "I'll let it go. For now. So why don't we do something safe, like have you introduce me to your horses?"

Owen's demeanor visibly changed. His shoulders relaxed, the lines in his forehead faded, and before her stood a new man. Who would have thought that one simple question would have made such a difference?

"It would be my pleasure," he said. He led her into the barn, which was clean and bright. It was obvious he took great pride in the space as it appeared well cared for. Not that Laura knew all that much about barns, but it was nothing like she'd imagined. She'd thought of barns as dirty, smelly places. But the dirt floor here was swept clean. The pungent aroma of hay filled the air and everything seemed to be neatly put in its place. Most homes couldn't boast such cleanliness.

"This is quite the space," she said, still looking around.

"My uncle was a most particular man. And since he taught me everything I know about animals, I suppose it's only fitting that I carry on his legacy. Plus having a clean barn stops the spread of disease. I know not everyone agrees with that idea, but I believe that's the case in all things. It's good to have a clean environment."

In her time with Owen, Laura had noticed that he always took special care to keep things as neat and tidy as possible. She appreciated that about him since James had always been the sort of man to leave everything lying all over the place, expecting everyone, especially her, to pick up after him. It was a pleasant change to see a man who believed differently.

Owen paused at a stall door. "This here is Troy's stall. He thinks he's king of this castle."

As Laura came closer to the stall, the horse poked his head out. She recognized him as the horse they had ridden here. She patted his neck. "So you're the trusty stallion who brought us here. It's nice to meet you officially, Troy."

Owen chuckled. "Actually, he's a gelding. And don't flatter him too much. He'll get a bigger head than he already has. Don't know how the horse got so puffed up, but he sure thinks a lot of himself."

Laura had never heard anyone speak of horses as though they were human beings. At least not in this way. She thought of them as animals, useful for many things, but not as having personalities or feelings. She thought the girls' treatment of Henry the rooster was a mere lark that everyone indulged. But from the way Owen spoke of his horse, Laura began to wonder if animals having feelings was an idea that the entire household believed in.

Troy whinnied and snorted, then tossed his head. As though he knew her thoughts. Like he was telling her not to underestimate him. Now she was the one getting silly.

"Here, give him one of these." Owen handed her a piece of the carrot.

Laura stared at it. "What do you mean, give it to him?"

Owen smiled at her in the indulgent way he smiled at his children. "Like this."

He held out his hand with the carrot on top of it, and the horse gently nibbled at it, then ate the carrot. Laura did the same, but when the horse's lips were moving over her hand, it felt funny, so she jerked her hand away.

"Easy now. Don't let him know you're afraid. Keep your hand flat and still. He won't bite you if you do that."

Owen picked up the carrot she dropped and set it back in her hand. She did as he told her, and let the horse take the carrot. Troy quickly gobbled up the treat, and she took her hand away.

"See there? You did just fine."

It had been a long time since Owen had spoken to her in such a gentle, kind and approving manner. Something in her heart swelled, reminding Laura of the good times they'd shared. Was it possible that this might be a new beginning between them?

"You haven't been around animals much, have you?"

Laura shook her head. "My family has always been in the hotel business. When you own a successful chain of hotels, it isn't good business to have many animals around. Horses were simply necessary transportation. As a child, I wanted to learn to ride, but my parents thought that it was unseemly for a young lady. When I married James, he wasn't willing to give me the kind of freedom that riding a horse would provide."

She didn't admit to many people that she couldn't ride, given that in Leadville, she didn't need to. She had enough money that she could afford a carriage of her own. Learning to ride a horse hadn't been a priority. But as she saw the pity on Owen's face, she wished she'd given a different answer.

"That's a shame," he said. "Knowing how to handle horses is a skill I think everyone should have. True, you have your hired help to do it for you, but you never know when you might run into an emergency situation. Can you hitch your own team? Saddle a horse? Stay astride by yourself?" He obviously knew the answers, but listening to him tick off his list made Laura feel more helpless than ever. Like the woman she'd been when she first met Owen.

Then Owen smiled. "You picked up things quickly when I taught you how to shoot a gun. Are you open to learning these things, as well?"

Laura stared at him for a moment. She'd felt like nothing but a bother since she'd come to the ranch, yet he seemed very open and willing to help her once again.

"I wouldn't want to be any trouble," she said.

Owen shrugged. "It's no trouble. If I'm going to protect you, these are important things for you to learn so I can keep you safe. It's highly unlikely, but if James shows up here, and we need to make a quick getaway, it will be easier if I know you can ride."

Laura felt a twinge of disappointment at his words. While she was glad that it wasn't a burden, it still stung that his generosity had more to do with protecting her than it did with his kindness of heart.

"Plus," he said, "I think you like animals. I remember, when we were waiting for James's trial, there was a stray cat that kept coming around, and you would give it bits of your food. Only an animal lover would do that."

Laura smiled. "I caught you feeding it from time to time, as well."

Owen shrugged. "I've always liked animals."

One more thing the two of them had in common. Sometimes it seemed as though they were similar enough that they should be able to get along better. Why things were different between them now, she didn't know. She'd become the woman she thought he'd been trying to help her become. Only it seemed he didn't like her now that she was no longer as biddable as she'd once been. Or maybe back then, she hadn't noticed how forceful he was. Compared to James, Owen was still a very gentle man. But given time away from James, on her own, Laura had realized her own strength. It no longer felt good to have a man pushing her around.

Owen gestured toward another stall. "This is Beauty, Lena's horse. A moody mare that only seems to listen to Lena."

As if the horse understood Owen's words, Beauty looked out of the stall and whinnied.

"Don't feed her," Owen said. "She bites for the fun of it."

Laura stared at the horse, who looked so innocent, but as she started to reach her hand forward to pet Beauty, the horse bared her teeth at her as if to tell her not even to bother trying.

Owen chuckled. "She is ornery, which I think is why Lena loves her. Lena always had a heart for the difficult ones. She puts up with me, after all."

With a grin, Owen led her to another stall. "Now

this here, this is Rascal, and if you'd like to try riding, I'd put you on her. She's Anna's horse and as gentle as can be."

Laura reached out to pet the horse, who whinnied at her, then reached her head forward for more. As Laura leaned into the horse, Rascal nuzzled her, and Laura couldn't help but wrap her arms around Rascal's neck.

"She's so sweet," Laura said, inhaling the fresh horse scent.

Owen nodded. "Yes, she is."

Then he pointed at another stall. "Daisy, Emma's horse, is in there. She won't behave unless Rascal is with her, but she's a good fit for Emma."

"It's so nice how you've figured out the personalities of the horses, so you know who works best with everyone."

"I like to match the rider to the horse. It makes all the difference."

The approving way he looked at her made Laura feel safe and warm. Like all the things she held against him no longer mattered. Could they spend the rest of her time at the ranch in peace?

And when it was over, even if these sweet moments made her think they might at least be friends, she would do her best to remember that Owen was just doing his job.

Owen couldn't stop smiling as he watched Laura interact with Rascal. He'd known Laura had a tender side with animals, but seeing her now, with her guard lowered, it deepened his admiration for her. Her quiet inner strength, particularly as she faced yet another challenge, another unknown, was something few people had, especially with all she'd endured.

Most people broke under the kind of treatment she'd received during her marriage to James. Watching her give her heart away to an animal melted Owen's.

"Would you like to learn to ride her?"

He watched Laura's shoulders straighten as she drew in a deep breath.

"I believe I would," she said, sounding just as resolute as she had when he'd asked her if she wanted to learn how to shoot a gun. White-knuckled, Laura had gripped that gun as if her life depended on it. But with every shot, both her hands and expression had become steadier. By the time they'd finished, she'd been able to hit every target. Not perfectly, but enough that he'd felt confident in her ability to handle the weapon.

Teaching her how to ride a horse would be the same thing. Only in this lesson, he would hopefully give her a skill that would not only be useful, but enjoyable, as well.

Owen walked over to his tack room and got out Rascal's halter and rope.

"I don't believe in putting someone right on a horse," Owen said as he returned to Laura's side. "You need time to get used to being around the animal, and you also need to learn about its care. I have a rule that if you ride it, you take care of it."

Laura nodded. "That sounds fair."

As Owen opened the stall door, he motioned for Laura. "For now, I prefer you not go into the stalls by yourself. But I want to show you how to catch a horse. My horses are all in stalls in the barn, but I'll also show you how to do it if you're working with a horse that's in the pasture."

Laura's eyes were on him as he slipped the halter over Rascal's head. Rascal was also probably the easiest horse to deal with. Gentle and eager to please, Rascal was the perfect horse for a beginner.

"That looks easy enough," Laura said.

Owen smiled. He had no doubt that she'd quickly master the task.

"Now you try," he said, slipping the halter back off.

As Owen handed her the halter, his hands brushed Laura's, and he felt the same spark he had back when he'd first protected her. He looked away in case Laura noticed anything different about their interaction or his reaction.

But just as quickly, he turned his attention back to Laura. This was no time to get distracted. Even if it was in the attempt to not feel whatever seemed to be between them from time to time.

That was the biggest problem with any attraction he might have for her or vice versa. None of those feelings were real or lasting. They seemed to be, but once the heat of the impending danger was gone, so, too, was the spark.

Laura slipped the halter on Rascal with ease, just

as he'd suspected she would. He showed her how to adjust the fit to make sure nothing was rubbing.

"Want to lead her out?"

Though it seemed like a stupid question, one of the things Owen had liked about the way his uncle had taught him about horses was that he'd eased him and Lena into all of their lessons. He didn't want Laura to feel forced into doing something she wasn't ready for. Not when she was dealing with a thousand-plus-pound animal whose brain didn't follow the same logic as a person.

Laura smiled at him. "I'd like that, thank you."

"Good. We'll just lead her out of the barn and walk her around the yard a little. Watch her movements and get a feel for her rhythm. If you can, walk next to her, talk to her and give her reassuring pats. The more she gets a sense of you, the more she learns to trust you."

Once again, Laura took his advice to heart, speaking to Rascal in such gentle and sweet tones that even Owen felt relaxed at her words. But it didn't surprise him. Laura had such a kindness and softness to her that it was no wonder his animals had taken to her so readily.

Which was why it had been so frustrating when she'd been so contrary with him when he'd first told her about James. Owen had been trying to save her life, and all Laura had wanted to do was argue and extract explanations. Here she simply did as he asked.

What was the difference between the contrary woman he'd brought here the other day and the old Laura, who seemed to have returned?

Perhaps he shouldn't even ask. Not with the sweet smile filling her face and the way all of her cares seemed to have left her shoulders.

That was what he loved about being here at the ranch.

Everyone seemed to have a similar experience, like the ranch was a different world without worries or cares. True, you still had chores to do, animals to care for, and ordinary day-to-day responsibilities. But they seemed so much more pleasurable with the fresh mountain breeze in your hair.

Winters left much to be desired, but Owen also didn't mind those so much either, snug in the house with his family and a crackling fire to keep them warm.

"Papa!"

Owen turned to see the girls standing on the porch. He smiled and waved at them. They quickly ran to him.

"Are we going riding?" Emma asked.

"What's she doing with my horse?" Anna asked.

He couldn't help but chuckle at the questions. Both girls would spend all of their time on a horse if they could, which was one of the reasons he didn't regret leaving town. There, the streets were too rough to let the girls ride, so they would have to plan outings to areas outside of town, which was a stressful process for both him and Lena. Lena, because she felt the need to pack enough food and water to last them a week, even if they were only going for an afternoon. Him, because with his work, he was always on guard, watching, looking for the criminal element. Despite all of Leadville's boasts about being a modern town, the lawless element was much greater than many of the other towns he'd been in. Owen had never felt like he could relax or put down his guard, even for a minute.

Laura also turned in the direction of the girls. "Your father was just teaching me about horses. I never learned to ride, so he's giving me a chance now."

She spoke to them like they were any other human beings, something he appreciated because he hated people who treated children according to the adage that they should be seen and not heard.

"You came here on a horse," Anna said.

"I rode with your father."

"How do you get places if you can't ride a horse?" Emma said.

"I would walk or take a carriage."

The girls looked at each other, then Anna asked, "Why didn't you take a carriage here?"

Owen drew in a breath, hoping that Laura understood that his children had been kept in the dark about the danger she faced.

"I believe your father thought it best not to take my carriage."

Two sets of eyes turned to him. Laura gave him a smirk like she knew he'd been worried about her answer and was quite pleased with herself for having turned the tables on him.

"Why didn't you want to take Laura's carriage?" Anna asked.

Before he could answer, Emma said, "We've never been in a carriage. Is it a fancy carriage? I'm sure it's more comfortable than our old wagon."

The girls could be relentless in their questioning. Especially with the put-out way Emma looked at having been deprived of Laura's carriage.

"I wanted to get home quickly. Carriages are much slower than just a horse," he said, careful not to lie. Even though he wanted to protect them from the truth, he always tried hard not to lie to his children.

As they often did, in unison, the girls asked, "Why?"

Owen stepped forward and put his arms around them. "You know why. I hate being away from you."

The girls rewarded him with snuggles, and he could honestly say that he'd told them the truth. He'd hung up his badge for a lot of reasons, but the most important had been that he wanted to be with his family. He hated hearing about everything they did in his absence, especially milestones he'd missed.

They'd already grown up so fast in their six short years, and he didn't want to miss any more time with them.

Emma pulled away first, then stared at him with those beautiful blue eyes he loved so much. "But we really want to ride in a carriage."

"It's not my carriage to be giving rides in." Owen smiled at her, then turned his attention back to Laura, who stood patiently holding Rascal. Though she seemed like she was doing fine while he'd been distracted, he needed to be more present with her.

"You're doing great. Don't mind them. They get an idea in their heads, and they won't let go."

Laura patted Rascal's neck. "Thanks. I'm having fun. Perhaps, since Anna is letting me use her horse now, when you all come to town for a visit, you'll allow me to repay the favor by giving the girls a ride in my carriage."

"Really?" The girls jumped up and down and clapped as they looked at each other.

"Really." Laura smiled at them with the same indulgence he or Lena might have done. "It's not as fancy as some carriages you might have read about, such as the famous Mr. Tabor's, but it's quite comfortable and, I'm told, fashionable."

Owen had heard about Horace Tabor's gold carriage. One of the early residents of Leadville and, some said, one of Colorado's richest men, he'd earned a fortune from the mines in the area. Though he no longer spent much time in Leadville, preferring his mansion in Denver, the town still rippled with stories about him. Especially on the few occasions when he did come to town.

The girls gave a small cheer, the sudden loud noise causing Rascal to jump.

Before Owen could grab the halter to calm her down, Laura had already tightened her grip on the rope.

"It's all right, girl," she said, reaching out to steady Rascal. "It's all right."

And just like that, Rascal settled. True, Rascal was

the least flighty horse he knew, but for someone as inexperienced around horses to learn so quickly…

Laura was something special.

He'd always known that and yet, the more he saw evidence of it, and the more he admitted it, the more he wished this wasn't just a case, that they could have something for real.

But that was the kind of wishful thinking that had him married to the wrong sort of woman the first time. The only good thing that had come out of that union was the girls, so he refused to regret that decision. But he also wasn't going to make the same mistake twice.

Chapter Six

The next day Owen declared Laura ready for her first actual riding lesson. After she'd walked the horse around the yard, the girls had helped Owen teach Laura how to groom and saddle Rascal. The lessons seemed to be slow, but as Laura watched how patient and gentle Owen was in the process, she appreciated his method. He wanted her to be comfortable with everything about the riding.

So why hadn't he taken that approach to getting her out here in the first place? It was like there were two Owens. This kind, gentle man, and then the forceful one who'd come to her boardinghouse the other day.

The girls had left Laura holding Rascal while they went to put away the items they'd used to groom the horse. Owen stood nearby, watching her.

"Am I doing all right?" Laura asked, turning to him.

She was rewarded with a smile. "You are. You've

taken to being around Rascal like a duck to water. If you're afraid, you're not showing it, and that's a good thing."

If she was afraid of anything, it was of disappointing him. Or doing the wrong thing to make Owen think she couldn't be trusted around horses. She gave the chestnut mare a pat, and Rascal whinnied.

Anna ran over to Laura, her face filled with delight. It was hard not to smile at such joy in a child.

"Are you going to try to ride today? Papa said he'd talk to you about it while we put everything away."

"I believe I am." Laura felt confident in her answer.

Anna regarded her with solemn eyes. "You don't have to be scared." She reached forward and patted Laura's arm gently. "I talked to Rascal, and I told her that she is to be good to you because it's your first time. She said yes."

Was there anything more endearing than a little girl who wanted to help Laura feel safe? She wasn't scared, but she couldn't dismiss the kindness of a child.

"Thank you very much. I appreciate that. It's so good of you to be watching out for me."

Anna nodded. "It's our family way."

Then the little girl abruptly turned and ran in the direction of the house. "Emma! When are you going to get out here with that rooster? Auntie said she'd only watch him for a little while."

The door opened and Emma came out, the rooster trailing her with what appeared to be some kind of leash on him. Emma was tossing out breadcrumbs, and the rooster followed, eating them.

Laura looked over at Owen. "What is that?"

Owen shook his head in the way he did when he seemed exasperated with the girls but was doing his best to go along with them. One of the things she loved about him as a father. "The girls were afraid the rooster would run away if they let him outside. Apparently, he hasn't taken a liking to learning manners."

Laura had watched the girls work with the rooster. At first, she'd been afraid that, because they were children, they might be torturing the poor creature. But the more she observed them, the more she noticed that they took the same gentle approach with the rooster as Owen had been taking with Laura and acclimating her to the horse.

True, the rooster didn't seem to like any of it, but as he walked around the yard with the girls in some kind of leash-and-harness contraption, he wasn't squawking like he was in pain. Actually, he didn't even seem that put out. Mostly he just seemed annoyed when he'd go one direction, and the girls would gently ask him to take another.

"Can you imagine?" Owen shook his head as he grinned. "Who would've thought you could train a rooster?"

"Does that harness thing hurt?"

Owen turned in the direction of the girls and the rooster and observed them for a moment before answering. "I was concerned at first because I didn't want them to hurt him. I helped them make the adjustments necessary so that the rooster wouldn't be harmed. They know not to jerk too hard, and if I see them doing anything that seems cruel, the rooster goes back in the henhouse."

It didn't seem like the girls were tormenting the rooster, especially since now and then one of the girls would give the rooster a reassuring pat. Just like they did with horses. They'd clearly spent a lot of time with their father and the animals, so it was no wonder they were taking the same approach to taming a rooster.

Owen returned his attention to Laura and patted the horse beside her. "Now let's get you going."

Owen helped her onto the horse, and even though she could've done it all herself, Laura felt it comforting to have Owen so strongly supporting her. His hands were gentle and warm, and she couldn't help but think of how safe they made her feel. James had cold, hard hands, and they always seemed to be used in violence. From hitting her to tearing open things with no regards for their contents. Sometimes the little gestures were the most telling.

The longer she stayed with Owen, the more she wondered if she had been too hasty in judging him for the forceful way he handled her at the boardinghouse. He hadn't physically harmed her, nor had he physically threatened her. And even now, she couldn't see him as being violent.

Could she let go of that one fight?

As Owen explained to her how to adjust her seat, and how to hold the reins, Laura wondered how she'd ever seen this gentle giant as a threat. Of course,

James had also been kind and mild mannered before the wedding.

"Now lean forward, make a noise like I showed you and gently squeeze your legs against the horse's belly."

Laura did as he asked, and was rewarded by Rascal taking a few steps forward. Owen had told her that while many people thought that to get a horse to go, you had to kick it, most horses, at least the well-behaved ones, just needed a gentle encouragement to go forward.

Rascal continued moving as Owen walked beside them. With each step the horse took, Owen gave them more room, making Laura feel more confident that she was riding the horse all on her own.

"You've got it," he said. "You're a natural."

The praise made Laura sit up straighter in her seat. She could feel herself relaxing with Rascal's gait, and enjoying the movement of the horse.

Anna came running to them. "You did it," she shouted.

Rascal's ears pricked up, and she gave a little jump. Laura tried to remember what she was supposed to do, and she pulled on the reins, but Rascal shook her head and gave another hop.

"Rascal!" Anna shouted, waving her arms.

The girl's chastisement seemed only to anger the horse more. Before Laura knew what was happening, Rascal took off on a run. Attempting to remember what Owen had told her about keeping calm, Laura tried to relax her hold on the reins, only they slipped through her fingers, and she lost her grip on them. The reins flapped against the side of the horse, but Laura couldn't grab hold of them again.

Rascal jumped and went even faster. Laura grabbed the saddle horn and held on as tightly as she could. As Laura tried to steady herself to stay on the horse, she could feel her heart pounding. Rascal was no longer bucking or doing anything crazy, just running. Laura could see Lena coming toward them, waving her arms. Rascal turned, and Laura could see Owen standing nearby. As Rascal ran toward him, Owen grabbed a loose rein and brought Rascal to a halt. At the jarring stop, Laura was finally able to catch her breath.

"Are you all right?" Owen asked, concern lining his face.

Laura nodded. "Surprised. I think if I knew what I was doing, that would have almost been fun. There was something exhilarating about going so fast. But I didn't like being out of control."

As she saw the doubt on Owen's face, Laura added, "I would like to be able to do both."

There had been a certain freedom in the speed at which Rascal had gone. In the short moments of Rascal's flight, Laura's hair had come loose. It was now flapping in the breeze. Everything about her felt ruffled, and she was sure she looked quite the sight. And yet, Laura had never felt so free.

"I can teach you to go fast, but let's master the basics first." Owen handed her the reins again. "First thing, don't drop your reins."

His smile made her wish things were different between them. Sometimes she could almost fool herself into believing this was genuine. Were they friends? Could they be friends? As his hands brushed hers to give her back the reins and show her how to hold them properly, the warmth she felt made her wish for something more. It seemed wrong to even entertain the idea. Not just wrong, but foolish. She was a fool to believe that there had been anything else between them. Believe wasn't even the right word. Hope, wish, maybe even dream. Because he'd given no evidence that he had any of those ideas for himself.

So what was this happening between them? All on her side again, she supposed.

Owen continued to make his lack of personal feelings for her clear and couldn't have been plainer when they'd spoken. It made her seem all the more foolish for feeling the things that she felt.

She gave Owen a nod, and he stepped away. Once again Laura asked the horse to move forward, and Rascal obeyed. This time, they walked around the yard at a slow and easy pace. They hadn't gone far when Rascal had run off on her, and it hadn't lasted as long as it had felt. It didn't take long for them to go the same distance at a walk. From time to time, Laura would reach down and pat Rascal.

"Good girl," Laura said giving the horse another pat. It was such a beautiful day, and Laura could see why the ranch was so much more appealing to Owen than the city. Here, they were far removed from the smoke of the smelters, the noise of all the people and the way the air seemed always to be full of something unpleasant. Until now, Laura had never considered the air in Leadville foul. But here at the ranch, where everything was so clear, she understood the difference. Understood why Owen would leave a successful career as a lawman to become a rancher. She hadn't asked him, and he hadn't volunteered the information. But now, she wasn't sure if they even had to have that conversation.

Laura chuckled to herself. They hardly had any conversation at all. If it weren't for Owen teaching her about the horse, she wasn't sure he'd even be talking to her.

Circling, Laura returned to Owen, who looked pleased. Why did her heart always have to jump at that sight?

"You did great," Owen said. "You looked very comfortable."

Lena approached them, also smiling. "Indeed you did. I'll admit I was nervous when Rascal took off on you like that. She usually isn't one to spook, and Anna knows better than to come running and yelling in the direction of the horse. I can assure you that she got quite the talking to, and it won't happen again."

"I'm sure that wasn't necessary," Laura said. "She's only a child, and she meant no harm."

"But she did know better," Owen said. "Here, around the animals, it doesn't matter what you mean to do. Rules are rules, and they're in place for a reason. The most important being for safety."

He held the horse for her, and Laura dismounted. Riding a horse was much easier than she'd thought it would be. Then Laura remembered how sweetly Anna had tried to encourage her, and she realized that many people found riding a horse for the first time a challenge. But maybe it had been so easy for her because of how long she'd wanted to try.

Once she dismounted, Laura gave Rascal another pat. "Thank you for being such a good sport. I hope we can do it again soon."

The girls approached, each of them carrying flowers. Anna held out her bouquet to Laura. "I'm sorry I scared Rascal with you on her. I hope it didn't upset you too much. I just got so excited that I forgot. I know I need to do a better job of paying attention when I'm around horses."

With every word, Anna had looked at Lena, who had probably told her word for word what to say. But the little girl truly looked regretful, and Laura knew it wasn't just because she got in trouble. She accepted the bouquet with a smile, then brought the flowers to her nose to smell. They were every bit as pretty as the ones she'd picked herself the other morning.

"What a lovely apology. Of course I accept. And such beautiful flowers. I love them. I hope we can find a vase or something to put them in. That way everyone can enjoy them."

Emma held her flowers out to Laura. "You should take these, as well. Anna's bouquet isn't very good, but that's because I stole the best flowers."

Emma smirked while Anna scowled, and the other two adults just shook their heads. It was sweet to be included in such a normal family routine, but as Laura took the second batch of flowers, her heart ached at the thought that such a cozy family scene would not be in her future.

"Thank you, Emma. Both sets of flowers are quite nice."

Emma seemed to ignore Laura's attempt at boosting Anna's morale, and turned to Lena. Though Anna smiled shyly at Laura as Emma spoke. "Now may we please go on our picnic?"

Lena sighed. "I didn't hear you invite Laura."

The girls turned back to Laura. "Would you like to come on a picnic with us?"

Laura had already known that a picnic lunch was on the schedule for today. She didn't want to admit it, but she'd heard Owen and Lena arguing about it before breakfast. "Of course I would. Thank you for asking."

The girls smiled, but Owen shook his head.

"No one's going anywhere until we get this horse put away."

Anna grabbed the reins and pulled the horse in the direction of the barn. "Come on, Laura. We need to get Rascal unsaddled and brushed so we can get on our picnic. If you ride the horse, you're supposed to put it away all by yourself. But sometimes, when we're in a hurry, Papa helps us. I'm going to help you today."

Once again, Laura's heart was warmed by the sweet child who felt a sense of empowerment at being able to help Laura and teach her about her horse. Children had always liked her, and she'd always liked children. What a shame this little girl didn't have a mother. But she did have an aunt who was like one, and Laura admired Lena for the way she loved those two little girls as her own.

Laura followed Anna into the barn and was impressed at the dexterity with which the little girl undid all the fastenings of the saddle.

Then Anna turned to her. "I'm not big enough to take the saddle off all by myself, so you get to do that."

Laura smiled as she did as the little girl asked, noting that Anna's eyes were on her the entire time. The saddle was heavy and bulky, but Laura had been expecting that. Owen had made her saddle the horse. He'd given the same explanation about knowing how to care for the animals you used.

She carried the saddle back to the tack room and put it back the way Owen had shown her. Even though Laura had done a good many things for herself since leaving James, this felt like one more victory of claiming her independence. True, she'd done so with the aid of a child, but now Laura knew she could saddle and unsaddle a horse by herself. She didn't have to ask a man to do it for her. And, even though she wouldn't be able to ride like Owen, Laura understood the basics of riding, and that was progress.

When she returned home, she'd go down to the livery and ask about getting a horse that she could ride. Owen was right. Riding was one more skill that would strengthen her ability to be on her own.

She turned and saw him standing in the doorway, light filtering around him so that he was merely a shadow. How she longed to run to him and tell him about this amazing discovery. To thank him for giving her one more piece of her dignity back. But he probably wouldn't value the gesture as much as she would. To him, it was just one more practical aspect of life on the ranch. Just another part of his job.

How could a man mean so much to her when she'd been working so hard at steeling herself against letting him into her heart? And how could he make it into her heart so easily when he'd made it clear that was the last place he wanted to be?

Neither of them had begun this time together with any intention of things getting personal between them, but somehow it seemed to be where they kept falling.

Or was that another sign of Laura's poor judgment?

Clearly, she needed to be just as focused on the task at hand as Owen was, avoiding these thoughts.

Laura brushed the dust off her skirt and grabbed the comb they used to brush the horses after a ride.

As she passed Owen, she said, "Thank you again for letting me ride Rascal. I truly enjoyed it, and I hope there will be more opportunities for riding."

Owen gave a jerky nod. "I'm glad. It's a skill everyone should have, and it's good you're finally learning."

His words confirmed Laura's previous thoughts. No matter how close she felt to him, or how much she wished for them to be friends, he was just doing his job. All business, no heart.

Chapter Seven

Owen couldn't have been more proud of Laura as he watched the jubilant expressions dance across her face. He remembered when his uncle had taught him to ride. He'd felt the same way, like he could hold his head in the air and be proud of who he was. There was something about giving people a new skill that they could take with them for the rest of their lives that was so empowering. It's why he'd taught Laura to shoot in the first place. Too bad more victims couldn't have the same opportunity.

The excitement in her voice had made him want to hug her and pick her up and twirl her around like he did with his girls. But that was too intimate of a gesture, and he had to keep his distance. It was easy to entertain fantasies of a future, especially with someone as lovely as Laura. She was so good with his girls, and he appreciated the way she treated them with respect. He'd had so many women fawn over the children and talk to them like they were infants or dogs. The girls were smart, and Laura recognized that.

He watched as Laura patiently brushed Rascal, with Anna helping out. Anna chattered to Laura non-stop, something that wouldn't seem like a big deal to most people, but it always took Anna a while to warm up to someone new. There were still women they knew in town she didn't speak to at all.

Lena and Emma came toward them, carrying a picnic basket between them. Knowing Lena, it was full of all sorts of tasty treats, and while Owen still wasn't entirely sure about leaving the safety of the house, the meadow wasn't far, and there were plenty of places to hide in between should the need arise. Owen's gun felt heavy at his hip, reminding him that he had one other measure of safety. Though Lena liked to brag about his skill with a gun, Owen took no pleasure in using it. Shooting well was a skill born of necessity, something he'd learned to keep them from starving. A waste of a bullet meant a missed meal, so Owen had quickly learned to make the most of it. The skill translated well to law enforcement.

Anna led the horse over to him. "Is she cool enough yet?"

Owen smiled. Rascal hadn't been worked hard enough to get too hot, but he was glad that at least some of his rules were still deeply ingrained within his children. He made a show of feeling the horse's chest. Then he nodded. "She sure is. Go ahead and put her away."

Laura didn't pay much attention to him as she

passed by with Anna, intent on fulfilling her duty as Rascal's rider.

When they'd finished putting the horse away, Owen picked up the basket and led the family down the small path to the meadow.

Ordinarily, he'd have the horses grazing. But it was better to keep the horses close in case they needed to make a hasty exit. As they approached the meadow, something about it didn't feel right. But as Owen looked around for signs that anything was amiss, he could find none. The ranch was situated in such a way that he'd be able to see anyone coming from miles away. Even here in the meadow, which was the only reason he'd agreed to the silly picnic, he had a good view of the land between the ranch and the town in the distance. He'd seen nothing.

Lena spread the picnic blanket and set the basket on top. As she passed out the sandwiches, she smiled in a way that made Owen even more suspicious.

"I believe I forgot the lemonade," Lena said. "You all just start eating, and I'll go get it."

That's what had felt off. His sister was trying to matchmake again. True, the girls were still here. But Lena wouldn't be around to act as a buffer between him and Laura as she'd done at every meal and in the evenings in the parlor. She obviously sensed the attraction that Owen felt for Laura.

Sometimes he caught Laura looking at him in a way that suggested she was developing feelings for him. Had Lena noticed, as well? And thought that there might be something there? But neither Lena nor Laura seemed to understand that these were not the feelings of love. Perhaps Owen needed to remind Lena of how he'd already made that disastrous mistake.

Laura seemed oblivious to Lena's ploy. She smiled at Lena. "Do you want me to go with you? I could help."

"Oh, I've got it, thanks."

Before anyone could say anything else, Lena had dashed off in the direction of the house, leaving Owen alone with Laura and the two girls.

"Where's the rooster?" Laura asked.

Owen looked around. He told the girls that the rooster was their responsibility. But before he could give them a lecture on properly taking care of their animals, Emma piped up.

"He's in a time out. He wasn't behaving like a gentleman, so we put him in his basket and left him in the barn."

Lena had given the girls a large basket with a latch to keep the rooster in at night. If there was going to be a rooster in the house, it wasn't going to roam around unsupervised.

"What if he gets too hot in there?" Owen looked at the girls firmly. "Did you leave him plenty of water? Is he in the shade?"

The girls looked at each other with the guilty expressions of children who hadn't considered those things. Sometimes they got mad at him for having so many rules, but this was exactly why.

"Remember what I told you. You should always

make sure that every animal under your care has access to plenty of water at all times. You also need to make sure that in the winter you've thought about warmth. And in the summer, you've thought about keeping them cool."

He'd told the girls this before, but they were still young, so they couldn't be expected to remember everything.

"We're sorry, Papa. We'll do better next time," Anna said, looking chagrined.

Next to her, Emma nodded. "We're very sorry Papa."

Knowing that rooster, and the ruckus he'd caused already at night when locked in the basket, Lena would probably hear him when she got home. He wasn't sure if she'd rescue it and bring it back to them or send it to the henhouse. Even though she'd originally agreed to let the rooster in the house, he was starting to think she was getting sick of the bird.

"We'll see what your aunt decides to do with the rooster when she gets to the house." Owen gave the girls a firm look.

They knew that whatever Lena decided, he would back her up 100 percent. That was the deal they'd agreed to when Lena had first come to look after the children. They stood behind each other's decisions, and the rare times when they disagreed, they never let the children know it.

Owen reached into the basket to pass out the cookies Lena had baked.

"These cookies are delicious," Laura said, sitting on the blanket and looking as pretty as ever.

She looked genuinely happy, and if there was anything Owen could say that he wanted for her, it would be her happiness. He could still remember the scared, miserable woman who was convinced that if she testified against her husband, he would kill her. It had taken a long time to coax a smile out of that fragile exterior. Now here she was full of joy and laughter as she chatted with his daughters.

Moments like this made him wish he'd met Laura under different circumstances. Or that her past had been different. Not that she had anything to be ashamed of, but when a woman was broken as much as Laura had been, she needed so much fixing that Owen wasn't sure it was possible. Or, when she finally was whole again, she realized that the man responsible for her transformation wasn't necessary anymore.

Would Laura love him if she didn't need him? Would she still look at him with those doe eyes of hers once she could do everything for herself?

Maybe, but in Owen's experience, that wasn't what happened.

The girls finished the cookies and jumped up. "Papa, may we go pick some flowers?"

"Stay where I can see you."

As they left, giggling, Laura turned and smiled at him.

"They're such happy children. And very well behaved. You and Lena have done a remarkable job raising them."

He let his gaze wander to the girls as they chased each other in the meadow. They had probably invented a game to see who would get the best flowers. Though they were often cooperative, they also had a competitive streak. He supposed they came by that honestly, considering that's how he and Lena dealt with each other.

"I'm proud of them," Owen said, his eyes still on the girls.

He couldn't bear to look at Laura or her expression. It was probably full of sympathy and admiration. Most women thought him extraordinary for raising two girls on his own. And Lena even more so for taking on her brother and his children. But he hated that. Why would a man be so highly regarded for raising his own children?

"May I ask how long their mother has been gone?"

Laura's curiosity was only natural. And though he'd told her that their mother was off-limits, the question was one that many people asked. He was tempted to give the same answer he always gave—*a long time*—but out of the corner of his eye, he saw a mixture of fear and sympathy. The sympathy was understandable, but the fear?

She was afraid she'd crossed the line, afraid of how he'd react now that she had. A piece of her abusive past she would never be able to let go of.

As much as he didn't want to talk about it, he also

didn't want to be that man. Laura needed to know that she didn't have to fear everyone, especially him.

"They don't remember their mother. She left when they were babies. She said that she couldn't handle raising twins on her own with me gone all the time. I tried to be home more, but it wasn't enough. She was killed a couple years later."

Sympathy shone in Laura's eyes. "That must have been very difficult for you. I can see why you brought Lena in. How wonderful that she was willing to take care of them. Didn't she want a family of her own?"

He should have known that opening up would only invite her to ask more questions. Lena's life was Lena's life. He knew why she'd done what she did. And that was enough.

"I suppose Lena had her reasons. It's not my place to share them. But I will say that for us family is the most important thing. I suppose being an only child, you don't know what it's like to have a sibling who cares for you."

He turned his attention back to the girls. Even in the distance, he could see they'd found a butterfly, and were chasing it. The best thing he'd ever given them was each other.

"It's good you have twins then," Laura said as if she knew what he was thinking. "You're right. It was lonely growing up all alone. My mother had several miscarriages, and I had a brother who was stillborn. My parents were so afraid of losing me, that they put me in a protective bubble where I was never allowed to do anything where I might get hurt. Falling in love with James was the first decision I truly made for my-self about my life."

Laura plucked a blade of grass and stared at it for a moment. Then she looked over at Owen. "I suppose it sounds rather pathetic, but since divorcing him, I've become rather good at deciding things for myself. I didn't like how forceful you were with me that day in the boardinghouse, not giving me a choice. That's why the way you taught me to ride, giving me choices and letting me make the decisions, felt so good."

Owen wasn't sure what he was supposed to say. Was he supposed to apologize for wanting to keep her safe? He supposed that's what her parents had thought they were doing, too, but they'd gone overboard.

"I can appreciate that," he finally said. "But you need to understand, there is a time for giving people choices, and there's a time when you need just to do what you're told without asking a lot of questions."

His answer didn't appear to make Laura very happy, but making her happy wasn't his job. Her happiness was a bonus, but it was a lot like raising children. Sometimes the right thing wasn't what made everyone happy, but it was best for everyone in the long run.

"Thank you for telling me about your wife," Laura said. "I know you don't like talking about it, so I especially treasure the information, and I'm glad to know. Do the children ever ask about her?"

Sometimes Laura was just like one of the children. What was that saying? You give them an inch, and they take a mile? Owen shook his head. "They know she's dead. It seems especially cruel to tell them the rest."

Laura nodded. "I can understand. I suppose if their mother left when they were small, Lena is the only mother they remember."

Owen glanced at her, wishing she wasn't so easy to talk to. There was a reason he didn't talk about any of this, but Laura made him forget. "She is. The only reason they know any different is that they call Lena Auntie, and some of their friends thought it was odd that they have an auntie and not a mother."

Laura smiled at him. "That must run in your family. You've never spoken of your parents, but you've referred to your uncle and the things he's taught you a lot. I take that to mean that your uncle played a large role in raising you, just as Lena is raising the girls. He must have been a special person, just like her."

The innocent look on her face told him that she wasn't trying to pry, but her comment pointed to one more painful family secret he preferred to keep buried. One more reason that falling in love with Laura was a bad idea. Even though they called him uncle, their uncle wasn't really an uncle, but their mother's lover. Owen shook his head. He'd thought he married her. Only she'd neglected to tell him she was already married. He'd built this magnificent house for her, her children and the children he hoped to have with her. But it hadn't worked out that way. His uncle had tried to save a woman who didn't want to be saved, and he'd gotten stuck with a couple of children in return.

Instead, he said, "Something like that."

"I hope you'll trust me enough to someday tell me that story, too," Laura said, her eyes shining full of the kind of hero worship he'd seen from her before.

"We don't talk about those things."

Laura looked wounded, as he'd known she would. But what was he supposed to say? *Don't dig into my heart because sharing the deep parts of my life with you is only going to make it harder to let you go? That so many pieces of his past were too shameful to mention?*

Bringing her to the ranch had been a mistake. He didn't want to get to know Laura better, didn't want her to get to know his family. It would only make her leaving even more difficult. But when Lena had insisted and Will had backed her up, Owen had felt he had no choice. In her misguided way, Lena probably thought this was the perfect opportunity for Owen to fall in love. Why she wanted him to fall in love, Owen had no idea. They had both been burned, and both agreed on their futures. So what was Lena's game?

Owen looked in the direction of the house, trying to see if Lena was on her way back. She'd been gone long enough. Too long. And while he would be pleasant to her when she finally did return, he'd find a way to have words with her later.

Laura cleared her throat. "I'm sorry for bringing all those things up," she said. "You're obviously not comfortable talking to me."

The hurt in her voice was evident, and part of Owen wanted desperately to make it go away. But his job wasn't to keep her from hurting; it was to keep her alive. All this other stuff between them, it was just a distraction, keeping them from the task at hand.

"I don't mind talking to you," he said. He looked back over to the girls to make sure they hadn't gotten into any trouble. And to give him a moment's space to figure out what he could say to her that wouldn't encourage the blossoming feelings but would soothe the hurt he'd caused.

He finally turned back to Laura and said, "I don't like talking about personal matters, that's all. I'm a very private person, and sharing things about my life, especially my past, is never comfortable for me."

Few people in his life knew the details. Will did, but that was because they'd known each other a lot of years.

"Do you think the rooster is all right?" Laura asked, looking back at the house.

"The rooster?"

Though the change of subject was a welcome reprieve, Laura's choice of topics was a bit odd.

"I was just thinking about what you said about water and heat. I know the basket is well ventilated, but I'm feeling quite warm out here. I would hate for the rooster to be roasted before his time."

A small smile turned the corners of her lips at her joke. She might have chosen an odd topic, but Owen couldn't help but laugh.

"I don't know about the rooster," Owen said. "But I'm getting parched. I'm not sure what is taking Lena so long with the lemonade, but I'm starting to think that we should go check."

Laura nodded. "I agree."

As if to confirm that it was time to go, the girls came running back, their hands full of flowers. "Where's Auntie with the lemonade?" Anna asked, panting.

Emma nodded. "We're going to die of thirst."

Laura grinned as she shook her head. "Now you know how the rooster feels."

Owen couldn't help but laugh. Not only did Laura have a good sense of humor, but she was right. If they were all this thirsty, how much more so was that rooster? Hopefully, this would be a good lesson for the girls.

They quickly packed up the picnic things and started for the house. But as they crested the tiny hill that stood between the meadow and house, Owen heard a gunshot.

His stomach fell, and while part of him wanted to go and check on Lena, he had Laura and the girls to keep safe. The root cellar wasn't too far away, and Owen ushered them in that direction.

"Was that…?" Laura looked at him with fear in her eyes.

Owen shook his head. "This isn't the time to ask questions. I need you and the girls to get in the root cellar. Girls, you know the special word. Once you get in there, bar the door, and don't let anyone in unless someone uses that word."

Owen had heard too many stories about people using a lawman's children against him, so he and Lena had given the girls a special word to recognize that a person was safe to go with. As they approached the root cellar, he gave a quick glance to the stick that they kept propped against the door. Most people would think that it was to keep the door closed, but for Owen, it was a way to know if anyone had gotten in there. Fortunately, the stick was exactly where it was supposed to be, so he felt safe letting Laura and the girls go in unattended.

He ran toward the house, occasionally looking over his shoulder to make sure that Laura and the girls had followed his instructions. At least this time, she hadn't continued badgering him with questions. Maybe she finally understood. As soon as he saw the door close behind them, Owen picked up speed. Once he got to the big pine nearest the house, he stopped. Using it as cover, he pulled out his gun and looked around.

There were no horses, so clearly it wasn't an intruder. Owen felt his breathing return to normal as he reholstered his gun. Lena had probably seen a snake or something and done away with it. She was fearless, except when it came to snakes.

As he rounded the tree to the back of the house, he saw Lena coming out of the house onto the back porch, shotgun in hand.

"What do you think you're doing? You scared me half to death," he said, starting toward her.

Lena's pale face told him he shouldn't have been so harsh with his words. Owen ran to her. "What happened?"

Maybe it wasn't a snake, but a mountain lion or a bear or something else.

"He's here," Lena said quietly. "I saw him sneaking around the side of the house when I came back to get the lemonade. Went inside to grab my shotgun. I got a shot off as he rounded the corner, but I think I only winged him. He headed toward the barn. I grabbed some more ammunition from the house, but I've been keeping an eye out. He's still there."

At least the barn was in the opposite direction of where he'd sent Laura and the girls. But Owen's stomach twisted at the thought of James finding his way here. How had he known to come to the ranch?

"Did he say anything?"

Lena shook her head. "No. I just saw him trying to open one of the windows, and I asked him what he thought he was doing. He got scared and started to run, which is when I made use of my shotgun."

Owen's chest hurt. "You're sure it was him?"

Lena nodded. "Looks just like his picture."

Owen looked around. "How do you think he got here? Could you tell if he was alone?"

"Beats me. I wish I had something I could tell you. I just saw a man trying to break into our house, and I reacted."

Then Lena looked around. "Where's—"

"Everyone is safe in your old playhouse."

Owen was glad he and his sister shared a history that allowed them to communicate without revealing what they were talking about. In fact, it would only leave an eavesdropper more confused. Another good thing about being close to his sister.

Lena nodded. "Good idea. What do we do now?"

"Send a signal to town. I'll head to the barn."

"Not on your own, you won't. I'll cover you with my shotgun. You've got too many feet of open space between here in the barn, and I won't have you be a sitting duck."

They went through the house and out the front door to get to the barn without being in the open. At least for part of the way. When they got to the front door, Owen looked out, trying to see if James had noticed his arrival. And if he could ascertain James's position, so he wasn't walking into a trap.

Owen's hope was that James thought Lena was just some ranch woman defending her property and not realize that she was defending something far more precious.

Movement by the side of the barn caught Owen's eye. James was positioned by the wagon, hidden in the shadows, but Owen could see him. Not enough to get a clean shot off, but eventually James would get impatient and move to a spot that would be easier for Owen to get to.

In fact, as he watched the other man fidget in the shadows, Owen suspected that James didn't realize that Owen was there, watching. Catching James Booth might be easier than they thought. Owen turned and let Lena know his plan.

Chapter Eight

Owen had done it again. He'd dismissed her without even discussing her options. Yes, there had been a gunshot, but Laura could shoot. She could have helped.

Laura took a deep breath as she looked around the inside of the root cellar. The girls had shown her where they kept a lantern, and Laura had lit it, giving them light in the windowless space. The area was neat, and the shelves were full of supplies for the family.

A very nice place, if one didn't hate being in enclosed spaces with no light. She took another deep breath and tried to settle her nerves. Even though they'd barely entered the root cellar, she could feel the walls closing in on her.

James had locked her in the basement once, refusing to let her out until she'd signed some papers giving him access to part of her fortune. At first, she'd refused, but the longer she stayed there, alone in the dark with all sorts of strange noises, the more her mind played tricks on her and the more afraid she became.

It had taken two days for her to give in, and even though it seemed like a relatively short period of time, it had been enough to make her hate enclosed spaces forever.

The girls pulled out a blanket and started sorting their flowers. They seemed perfectly content here in the root cellar, but even with the light from the lantern, Laura's skin was starting to crawl.

"Do you do this often?" Laura asked, trying to find a way to stay calm.

Emma and Anna looked at each other, then shook their heads. "We've practiced several times," Anna finally said.

"But Papa is a scaredy-cat. He always thinks things are dangerous." Emma gave a dramatic sigh. "It's probably just another snake. Auntie hates snakes. She's always shooting them, and if Papa hears the gun, he makes us come here until it's safe."

Laura could relate to having an overprotective father. Most of the time, Owen seemed like a reasonable man. He was very patient with the girls, and took the time to make them feel comfortable. But clearly the forcefulness he showed with her wasn't limited to her.

At least the children didn't act afraid.

Whereas she was about to go crazy from being cooped up in here even for this short period of time.

Still, it seemed silly for Owen to turn something as simple as a snake into a big ordeal.

"How long does he make you stay in here?"

Anna let out a long sigh. "For ages. It's why we have a few toys and things in here. Sometimes Papa takes hours to check the whole perimeter."

The exasperated way Anna said *perimeter* and stumbled over the pronunciation, made Laura smile. Clearly Owen said the word often in front of his daughter. Though it was obvious they all loved each other very much, even the children got annoyed with their father's heavy-handed ways. Especially with the drawn-out way the little girl said *ages*. Laura knew Owen was concerned with his family's safety, but this seemed to be taking it a little too far.

As Laura replayed in her head the scene of when Owen told them to go to the root cellar, she didn't think they had anything to worry about. After all, she'd seen the house. It didn't appear as though anyone was there. No horse, no carriage, no sign that the threat was from a human being. And with the watchful way Owen had constantly looked out over the horizon, they would have seen someone coming.

"Maybe I should see if I can help them to make things go faster," Laura said, looking at the girls.

Emma shook her head. "I wouldn't do that if I were you. If you disobey Papa, he might send you to bed with only bread and water for supper."

Anna nodded. "And you don't get any butter or jam on it either."

Once again, Laura fought the urge to laugh. To the girls, this was a dire punishment indeed. But if that was the worst wrath one could expect from Owen, she would take her chances.

"Well, I'll be sure to tell him that you girls had no part in my leaving. But you mind your Papa, bar the door behind me and stay here as he instructed."

Wide-eyed, the girls nodded at her. Clearly, they were stunned that someone would go so far as to disobey their father. But Laura wasn't a child; she was an adult. And it was ridiculous that Owen continued to treat her like she was as helpless as his daughters.

Laura wasn't afraid of snakes. When she was a child and her parents refused to let her have a pet, she'd found a snake in the garden. She'd kept it hidden in her room, and she'd take it out to play with it. Had the snake not gotten loose, no one would have ever known. But sadly, it did. One of the chambermaids had found it in her room, and the results were not pretty. Since then, Laura had always had a soft spot for snakes. If no one else would like them, she would.

Laura unbolted the door and slipped outside. As soon as she closed the door behind her, she could hear the bolt slide back in. At least the girls knew what to do. It was just a shame that Owen had such a tendency to overreact.

As she walked toward the house, Laura caught a glimpse of a flash of light against metal. She turned in the direction of the light and saw Owen standing on the front porch behind a pillar, gun drawn.

All this over a snake?

Was he crazy, pointing his gun at the air?

Sighing, Laura drew closer to the house. Owen

must've noticed her movement because he turned in her direction. Though she couldn't see the expression on his face, she could see the shake of his head as he pointed back at the root cellar. Then he lowered his gun, seeming to aim it at the barn.

He shook his head again, then turned to the front door. She assumed Lena was standing there. He said something to the other person, and sure enough, a few seconds later, Lena stepped out the back door.

What was going on? For the first time, Laura had to wonder if maybe there was something dangerous out there after all. Some wild animal? If it were James, he'd have already been causing a ruckus.

She noticed that while Owen kept his gun pointed at the barn, he had turned his gaze in her direction. He whistled, then Lena ran to the pine tree that stood about halfway between the house and where Laura was.

Lena looked in Owen's direction, and Owen nodded. Then Lena gestured at Laura to come to her.

Laura ran to the tree, and when she got there, Lena said, "What do you think you're doing? Didn't Owen tell you to stay in the root cellar?"

Breathless, Laura nodded.

"Well, why didn't you listen?" Lena said, looking disgusted.

Having finally caught her breath, Laura said, "The girls said that he does this sort of thing all the time and it was probably a snake. It's ridiculous to have to stay in such an enclosed area over a snake."

Lena shook her head. "I suppose your ex-husband

could be considered a snake. But now he probably knows you're here. It's not safe for you to go back to the root cellar, so come with me to the house. On Owen's signal, run."

Before Laura could process Lena's words, Lena looked over at Owen, who nodded. As they ran toward the house, Laura heard the crack of a gun, then felt the force of being roughly shoved to the ground.

The weight of Lena's body on top of hers was heavy, almost too heavy, but then Laura heard Lena say softly in her ear, "Crawl. As fast as you can, stay low to the ground and crawl."

More shots rang out, and by now Laura had oriented herself enough to know that they were from Owen's gun. The first shot had come from a different direction. Laura moved as quickly as she could. She continued to crawl up the stairs across the porch and didn't stand until she opened the back door. Lena followed, but Laura noticed she was walking funny.

"Did you hurt yourself?"

Lena looked pale. "I've been shot. In the leg. I don't think it's bad. But it sure hurts. I'm going to sit here for a minute. You need to go to the front door, and if Owen is still standing there, you need to crack the door and tell him you're safe."

Laura looked at the other woman, who was growing paler and paler by the minute. "And tell him you've been shot," Laura said.

Lena looked at her with so much anger it felt almost as though Laura were the one with a gunshot wound. "Don't you dare tell him I've been shot. If he knows I've been hurt, he'll be distracted, and more people will be in danger. You tell him you're safe, and that's that."

Laura hesitated, and Lena shook her head. "I'm sitting here right now because you didn't listen. Don't make the same mistake twice."

As the import of Lena's words washed over her, the weight on Laura's chest was almost unbearable. Lena was right. Had Laura not come out of the root cellar, Lena wouldn't have been shot.

Swallowing the tears that threatened, Laura walked to the front door, peering out the tiny window to make sure Owen was there before cracking the door open.

"Lena told me to tell you that I'm safe."

"Where is she?"

Laura took a deep breath. Lena hadn't prepared her to answer any questions. It didn't feel right to lie to Owen, but she couldn't bear to cause any more trouble by telling him the truth.

"In the kitchen. She's busy with other things."

Owen gave a quick nod. "Good. You need to get to the store room and stay there this time. Tell Lena to cover me from the girls' room. He was hiding by the wagon, and ran into the barn."

They weren't going to be able to follow his orders, but Laura nodded as she said, "All right."

She'd take this information to Lena and let Lena decide what to do with it. But from the look on Lena's face, there was no way Lena was going to be able to help Owen.

Laura closed the door behind her and returned to the kitchen. Lena was still in her chair, but she'd found some towels and had wrapped them around her leg. Blood was already seeping through them.

"We need to get you to a doctor," Laura said.

"We need to do what Owen asked. What did he say?"

From the way the other woman clenched the side of the table, Laura could tell she was in pain. But the glare Lena shot her told her that she'd better not leave anything out. So Laura repeated Owen's words, knowing that there was no way Lena could do what she'd been told.

Lena reached for the shotgun she'd left on the floor when she'd crawled into the house. The grimace of pain she gave as she moved made Laura cringe. Especially because Lena couldn't support her weight to stand.

"You're not fit to do anything. You need a doctor."

"I've already sent the signal to town for help. That's the closest doctor. There's nothing we can do, except help keep Owen safe while he goes after James."

It looked like it hurt Lena even to say that much.

Laura picked up the gun. "I'll do it."

The disdainful look Lena gave Laura would have made Laura back down in the past. But that was the Laura James had known. To the new Laura, Lena's gesture only made her more determined to prove herself.

"Do you even know how to shoot?"

"Owen taught me."

Lena nodded slowly. "I suppose he would. Did you pick up learning how to shoot the way you picked up learning to ride?"

"I did." Laura squared her shoulders.

"All right." Lena let out a long sigh. "Help me up to the girls' room. I'll sit next to you and tell you what to do."

It was a struggle, holding the gun and giving Lena something to balance on as they made their way up the stairs. But Laura wasn't going to let on that she found it difficult. She knew that it had been hard enough for Lena to ask for help, let alone accept it.

When they finally got up to Emma's room, Lena pointed to a chair. "Pull that over to the right side of the window. I can see what I need from there."

Laura did as Lena asked, hating her labored breathing. But if the closest doctor was in town, what else were they supposed to do? Laura knew nothing about tending a normal wound, let alone a gunshot wound. The best she could do was trust Lena and pray that the other woman would be all right.

Once the women were in the positions Lena had indicated, Lena called out the open window, "I'm ready. Let's get this man."

"Did you get Laura out of the way?"

"Yup." Lena turned and winked at Laura.

"I hope you locked the door. That woman doesn't have a lick of sense. I don't know why she can't just listen."

Lena gave a half snort, half laugh, but shame filled

Laura. Is that what Owen thought of her? She supposed, since Lena was injured because of her, she
couldn't argue. But Owen didn't even know that. How
poorly would he view her when he found out about
Lena's injuries?

A high-pitched screech came from the barn.

"That sounds like Beauty," Lena said.

"It sure does." Owen adjusted his gun. "That may
be the distraction I need. I'm going in."

As he started down the porch steps, Lena nudged
Laura.

"Be ready," Lena said quietly. "When I tell you to
shoot, you shoot, no questions asked. I'm watching
for anything that could be movement from James or
his men. Even a slight delay puts Owen's life at risk."

Laura swallowed, willing herself to remain calm.
Though she'd always known the threat from James
was real, being in the middle of the action, with the
responsibility to protect someone else's life made the
situation seem even more frightening.

She'd trusted Owen with her life, and now he was
trusting her with his. Even if he didn't know it.

Owen darted from object to object, looking like
he was searching to make sure no one was hiding
between the house and the barn. He paused at the
wagon. He lifted the tarp, shook his head, then made
a motion to Lena.

The gesture seemed to mean something to Lena,
who leaned in to Laura and whispered, "The area
is clear. If James brought help with him, they aren't
nearby. He's going into the barn. No matter what hap-

pens, no matter what you hear, you do not leave this position, and you keep your gun ready until I say differently. Do you understand?"

It was almost insulting the way Lena kept pushing her point. Like she was rubbing salt in what would always be a wound between them.

"I understand," Laura said.

"Good."

As Owen went into the barn, Lena let out a long sigh and closed her eyes. Perhaps the other woman would rest now. But just as quickly as Lena had closed her eyes, she opened them again.

"If you need to rest—"

Lena glared at her. "I don't need to rest. I was praying. Asking God for His help in what should have been an easy situation, that now seems almost impossible."

Then Lena shook her head. "No. It will be fine. Owen has handled situations far more dangerous than this. I just hate not being able to help him. He's counting on me."

Once more, Laura's stomach twisted at Lena's words and the reminder that this was all her fault. "I'm sorry," she whispered, trying not to cry.

"We don't have time for that. You made a mistake. Don't let that ruin everyone's future. Move on and do better."

Only a fool wouldn't know Lena fought the pain with every word. But Lena was right. Laura's guilt wasn't going to save them. Not when they had to be alert in case they were needed. How Owen and Lena were able to push away their feelings so easily to do a job, Laura didn't know. But until they caught James, Laura was going to try.

Owen slipped into the barn, glad he knew all of the barn's secrets and had a way to get in without making noise or casting a shadow. James was in here, waiting. The back door, which Owen always kept open, was closed.

"I know you're in here," Owen called. From his vantage point, he could see the entirety of the barn. James was at a disadvantage. If he moved from his hiding spot, Owen would see him.

Owen listened for the sound of the other man moving. Even if he didn't answer, there would be other clues.

A horse whinnied in response.

"How'd you get here? I didn't see a horse."

The more Owen talked, the more confident James would feel about Owen's position, and the more likely he was to give away his own.

Beauty pawed at her stall. Her scream earlier had been what had given Owen the confidence to enter the barn. James was in Beauty's stall. Beauty didn't like men much, and she especially didn't like them in her stall. She barely tolerated Owen's presence, and even he knew not to turn his back on her.

The screech was a warning. The clunk of her hooves against the stall door another. And she didn't believe in third chances. James would either make his move soon, or Beauty would force him into it.

Owen listened to the rustling sounds of the other animals. They were anxious because they knew what he knew. No one liked to mess with Beauty.

"It'll be easier for you if you just give yourself up now. I'll put in a good word for you."

Not that it would help. James had killed two guards escaping from prison, and Owen didn't know the if the third had pulled through. There wasn't a judge on earth who wouldn't hang him. The trial would only be held to give a sense of fairness.

"I want my wife."

Owen shook his head. "Not going to happen. She doesn't want you. That's why she divorced you."

Men like James had egos bigger than the mountains that surrounded them. Owen's words would serve to antagonize him, which would force him out of hiding. And, hopefully, into a mistake.

"Is she your woman?"

It would be easy to say no because that was the truth. But this wasn't about the truth; it was about getting James to reveal his position with minimal bloodshed.

"What do you think?" Owen asked instead.

Silence. But now that Owen had been in the barn long enough to distinguish the subtle sounds of the animals, he could hear Beauty's nervous movements. James wouldn't be able to hide much longer.

"I think you made a big mistake."

Owen heard the latch of the stall door just as he heard Beauty make her move. She let out an angry screech, then James wailed in pain. Beauty must have bitten him hard and, from the loud thud, had probably kicked him, too.

As Owen moved in the direction of the stall, Beauty darted past him. It was tempting to catch the horse, but as angry as she was, she needed time to cool down. Lena would be better able to handle her. Beauty wouldn't go far.

Owen could see James struggling to get up at the stall entrance. He'd definitely been kicked, and probably bitten. The limp was a sure sign. James saw him coming and reached for the gun at his hip. But when James took a step toward Owen to get a clearer shot, he kicked over the basket sitting there.

The rooster came flying out, claws ready for battle. It didn't like being in the basket, and it sure didn't like being kicked over. It was enough of a distraction, as James swatted at it and tried to duck away from the razor-sharp nails, that James dropped his gun.

Unarmed, James would be easy to take down. Especially with a leg injury and the various cuts and scratches from an angry rooster and a biting horse. As Owen came toward him, James's eyes grew big and round. He knew it was the end.

"I'll tell you again. Give up easily, and I'll put in a good word for you."

"You know that's not going to happen. I won't go back to jail. Just give me my wife, and I'll be on my way."

Owen shook his head. "And I told you. It's not going to happen. Why make it harder on yourself?"

James looked like he was thinking about the offer,

but then he turned and went to Rascal's stall. He opened the stall door and whistled. Then he ran to one of the other stalls and did the same thing. Owen understood what he was doing. Trying to get the horses to create another distraction. With horses loose in the barn, and the only open entrance near Owen, they would naturally charge toward Owen in their startled state. Owen put his gun away and stepped aside. Of course he wouldn't shoot, knowing that the horses could make a sudden movement and take the bullet. But that didn't mean he was going to give up so easily either. Just as he had underestimated the amount fight left in James, James had underestimated the amount of fight left in him.

The horses raced past Owen, forcing him to step aside. Owen took a step toward James, and James picked up one of the lanterns and lit it.

"What do you want more? Me? Or your barn?"

The ploy to use the horses as a distraction had quickly failed, since Owen's horses had simply run out of the barn. It would be a challenge to catch them now, but later, when they got hungry, they'd come back on their own.

Which left Owen with nothing to fall back on but his gun.

He'd no sooner unholstered it than James dropped the lantern. Flames licked at the hay as James laughed and ran to the back door.

"You deserve to lose your barn."

Owen chased after him, knocking over one of the

water buckets near the flames in hopes it would slow the spread of the fire.

As James fumbled with the latch on the back door, Owen used the moment to take aim. He didn't like what he had to do, but this man had to be stopped. And with the smoke filling the barn, it had to happen now.

Just as Owen pulled the trigger, he heard a voice yell, "Owen!"

He jerked, and the shot went wide as Owen turned to Laura. Her face was white and fear filled her eyes.

When he turned back, James was gone. He'd jumped on Daisy's back and was riding away.

James might be gone for now, but he'd be back.

Chapter Nine

As soon as Owen turned toward her, Laura knew she'd made another terrible mistake. She hadn't seen James when she'd entered the barn, just the smoke, and Owen's back.

All she'd meant to do was get help for Lena, and now James had escaped.

The anger on Owen's face was evident, and nothing Laura could do was going to take it away. Especially once she told him why she'd stormed into the barn.

"Do you have any idea what you just did?" The angry words coming out of Owen's mouth made Laura shrink back.

She'd known he had a forceful side, but this anger? What would he do when she told him about Lena?

Laura shook her head. It didn't matter. Lena needed help.

"Lena fainted. She needs a doctor. She said the

closest one is in town, and she sent a signal for help, but I don't know how much time we have."

Owen stared at her. "Lena never faints."

"She was shot," Laura said quietly.

Owen looked around. "When? I thought James was alone."

This time, Laura couldn't help the tears she'd been fighting so hard to keep at bay. "When she came to get me."

She watched as Owen clenched and unclenched his fists. That was what James always did shortly before hitting her. Laura turned, knowing that the blow wouldn't be as bad if he couldn't get a direct hit. When she did so, she spied a bucket of water.

With the smoke still filling the barn, there wasn't time to do anything else. Laura grabbed the bucket and threw the water at the fire. Not waiting for Owen's response or actions, she ran to the next stall and grabbed that bucket of water.

When she went to dump it on the fire, she noticed that Owen had done the same thing. Fortunately, they'd refilled all the horses' water before going on their picnic. The water buckets were soon empty, and the fire still smoldered. Owen grabbed a shovel and started throwing dirt on it. When Laura looked around for another shovel, Owen pointed outside the barn.

"Get more water from the well. I'll keep using the dirt to keep the fire from spreading. Hurry!"

Laura hesitated as she tried to decide which bucket to use, and Owen shouted, "Now! This isn't the time to argue."

She grabbed the first bucket and ran to the well, letting the tears fall freely. Clearly Owen thought her just as stupid as James did. And maybe she was. It was her fault Lena had been shot. Her fault James had gotten away. Now they were putting out a fire that James had most likely set, and somehow that was all probably Laura's fault, as well.

The well wasn't far from the barn, and Laura was grateful that whoever had built the barn had the foresight to know that they'd need to bring in a lot of water. Probably not for fighting a fire, but it did make chores easier.

Her arms ached as she carried the water back to Owen. The fire looked mostly out, and Laura was glad that it hadn't had the chance to spread far. She handed the bucket to Owen, who dumped it on the remaining embers.

He turned and looked at her, his face full of the kind of angry emotions she was used to seeing on James's face. Owen hated her, and Laura didn't blame him. James used to torment her for ruining his life, but in Owen's case, she deserved the wrath.

"Where's Lena?"

"In the girls' room. She was telling me what to do while I covered you."

Owen made a noise. "If that gunshot wound doesn't kill her, I will."

Laura couldn't tell if he was joking or serious, but his words still traveled down her spine in a most uncomfortable way.

"Where was she hit?" he asked, turning toward the door.

"In the leg."

Owen gave a quick nod. "Stay here and make sure there are no flare-ups. If you see anything glowing, put more water on it."

"What about the dirt?"

He shook his head. "If there's any with hay in it, it'll fuel the fire. I know what to look for. You don't. Stick with the water."

Laura looked in the distance. "And James? What if he comes back?"

"He won't." Owen's shoulders relaxed slightly, like he believed they were safe and he no longer needed to be on guard. "He's injured and will need some time to recuperate before trying again. Even James isn't dumb enough to come back today."

If only Laura felt as confident as Owen. "He's smarter than you think."

"Smart or not, he's hurt and not capable of doing much until he gets his injuries treated. We have more pressing matters to attend to right now. If the fire flares up and spreads, there's more at stake than just our lives. The last thing we need is a wildfire."

Then he gave her a look filled with such disdain, Laura wanted to curl up in a ball and hide. "I know it's asking a lot since you seem completely unable to follow directions. But please, just do as I ask."

He looked almost defeated when he said those words. The condemnation Laura felt couldn't have been greater. She'd completely ruined his life because she hadn't listened to him, and there was nothing she could do to make up for it.

"I will," Laura said, then picked up the bucket to get more water.

She followed Owen out of the barn but stopped at the well while he continued to the house. Laura had no real sense of how far it was to town, or how long it would take help to arrive. But she'd do her best to help the Hamiltons for as long as it took.

Returning to the barn with the water, Laura carefully looked to see if there were any signs of the fire coming back. There didn't seem to be anything glowing red, but she wasn't going to leave it to chance. Her arms ached, her legs ached, and now her head was starting to ache. But she wasn't going to leave her post.

When she'd first been in the girls' room with Lena, Lena had paused to pray. In all the confusion, Laura hadn't even thought to do so. She thought of herself as a good Christian, but maybe she wasn't even good at that. Not when she'd made so many mistakes born out of her pride. She thought about where it said in Proverbs to trust in the Lord with all your heart.

As she stared at the smoke rising from the ashes, Laura had to admit that she hadn't trusted in the Lord at all. Not once since being told James had escaped had she gone to the Lord in prayer on the subject. She certainly hadn't prayed about how to handle Owen and his forceful attitude toward her. No, she'd just plunged headlong into what she thought was right, even though she had no experience in these matters.

She'd insisted on her own way, and even in a dangerous situation, Laura had thought of herself first.

Lord, I'm sorry.

They were the only words she could pull out of her aching heart, and they seemed so insignificant compared to the damage she'd done. Lena might die, and Laura could see that many of the boards in the barn would have to be replaced. To say nothing of the horses running wild out there. How they'd catch them, she didn't know.

And then there was the fact that James was still on the loose.

Who else would her ex-husband hurt before he was captured again?

Laura heard a noise behind her and she turned.

Owen stood in the doorway, exhaustion written all over his face.

"How is Lena?"

"She'll live. I got the bullet out, and it looks like it missed any major arteries. But she'll be off that leg for a while. I've got her bandaged up, and I gave her something for the pain and to make her sleep. She'll be madder than that stupid rooster when she wakes up, but she needs to take it easy and heal."

Then Owen looked around. "Speaking of that rooster, have you seen him?"

Laura stared at him, then glanced around. "No. Why?"

"I owe that bird a debt of gratitude." Owen sounded almost disgusted to have to admit it.

"How so?"

He made a noise as he shook his head. "He distracted James enough to get him to drop his gun. There are a lot of things you can plan for, but no one ever thinks a crazy rooster is going to attack."

Owen chuckled for a moment; then his face grew somber. "You need to know that I'm mad. Real mad. I can't ever remember being this angry. If you had just stayed put…"

He didn't need to finish his thought as he shook his head. Laura knew. If she'd obeyed Owen, none of this would have happened.

"I know," she said quietly. "I'm sorry."

His nod told her that while he understood she was sorry, he wasn't ready to hear her apology.

"I'm not one to accept excuses. But I have to know. What were you thinking, coming out of a safe place that I'd asked you to stay in after we all heard a gunshot?"

Put that way, Laura sounded almost reckless in her behavior. And from Owen's perspective, she could see why he would view her in that light.

Laura swallowed. "I was scared of the small space. The girls said it was probably a snake."

Her answer only made him look more disgusted. "You trusted six-year-olds over my word?"

Now she felt like she'd been completely ridiculous. Of course six-year-olds knew nothing about what it meant to be safe on a ranch. Laura shook her head.

No, they knew more than she did because they at least knew to listen to Owen.

"They said it had happened before," Laura said weakly.

He closed his eyes and pursed his lips in the way he did when he was particularly annoyed. "Did it ever occur to you that we might tell the girls things like 'It turned out only to be a snake' to protect them from the knowledge of what was really going on? This may be the first I've ever brought my work to the ranch, but that doesn't mean trouble hasn't come calling."

Could she feel any more stupid?

"I'm sorry." Tears rolled down her face as she shook uncontrollably. It hadn't been enough for her to have to come to terms with God over her willfulness. She deserved every bit of Owen's wrath.

Owen took a step toward her, and Laura shrank back. She might deserve what she got, but it didn't mean she'd accept the pain willingly.

But instead of continuing toward her, Owen turned away. He clenched and unclenched his fists, then spun back in her direction.

"You know, I'm trying to understand. To be patient with the fact that you've been hurt by a man time and again. But every time I come near you, you flinch. Have I once raised a hand to you? To my children? To anyone?"

His voice was raw and full of anger. But as Laura considered his words, she had to admit that he hadn't. Not even in protecting her. She'd never seen Owen resort to violence. True, she'd watched him almost shoot James, but that was part of his job.

"No," Laura said quietly.

Owen stared at her, hard. "I want you to remember that. You have put my family in grave danger. That would push many men over the edge. But I am standing here, trying to reason with you, trying to understand, and…"

He turned away, shaking his head. "I need to round up the horses and figure out what to tell the girls. You do what you've got to do, but I'd sure appreciate it if you'd make sure my barn doesn't burn down."

She'd thought he'd sounded defeated before, but now he sounded like he'd been crushed into the ground. Still, there was one more thing they hadn't considered.

"What about James? Are you sure he won't come back tonight?"

Owen stopped but didn't turn to look at her. "I doubt he's that stupid. He's been bitten and kicked by a horse and is walking with a noticeable limp. From what I could tell, the rooster clawed up his face pretty good, too. The excitement of the moment has worn off by now, and he's probably hurting pretty badly. I suspect he's gone somewhere to lick his wounds and figure out his next move."

Then Owen continued out of the barn. Laura would have liked to have found confidence in his explanation, but she had no confidence at all where James was concerned. Not that she would say that to Owen. She'd lost all credibility with him, and she didn't blame him.

* * *

From the dust swirling in the distance, Owen knew that help was on the way. For all the good it did him now. How had James gotten here undetected?

Troy came up to him and gave him a nudge. Owen patted the horse. "Hey, buddy. I knew you'd come back. Where are all of your friends?"

Some people might think it weird that Owen talked to his horse like he was a person, but Troy had been there for him through a lot of rough spots, and sometimes he thought the horse understood him better than most people. Definitely better than Laura did.

Owen tried to push her out of his mind. It didn't matter if Laura understood him or not. His only job was to protect her, and while he technically had been successful in that mission, her complete disregard for anything he told her was proving to be a liability. Maybe he needed to get someone else to do the job. But who?

As he mentally went through the list of men he knew, his gut twisted at the reminder that he'd promised. Laura probably didn't remember, or she'd at least gracefully let him out of it, but what did Owen have if he didn't keep his word? Lena would tell him to pray about it.

Owen's stomach sank even further. The bullet had come out easily, and the wound was clean. He'd doctored many a bullet wound in his day, and he hadn't killed a man yet. But this was Lena. He was supposed to protect his sister, not get her shot.

As he looked in the direction of the meadow, he

saw Rascal and Beauty grazing. They were probably happy to have the fresh grass for a change. But no Daisy. Daisy and Rascal were like two peas in a pod, kind of like the girls. That was part of why he'd gotten the horses for them. The horses hated being separated, and Owen liked the idea of having them watching over his children.

Hopefully Owen would be able to find Daisy when they found James so his daughter could have her horse back.

A loud crowing sound next to him made Owen jump. Then he smiled and bent to pick up the rooster. "Hey, Henry. You did good work today. Makes me glad you didn't end up in Lena's stew pot."

As he stroked the rooster, he felt the one spur he'd failed to cut off. "Sorry about that, old boy. I'm glad I didn't get it, because with your claws and that good spur, you might have saved my life."

Henry made what Owen thought must be a satisfied noise as Owen stroked him. "But if you hurt one of my girls, we might have to have a different conversation."

The girls! Owen still had no idea what he was going to tell his daughters, but they'd been stuck in the root cellar long enough. They didn't enjoy going in there, but it was the only way to keep them safe.

Carrying the rooster, he walked over to the root cellar and knocked on the door, then said their special word. The door opened, and Anna smiled at him.

"Oh good. Henry is all right. I was worried about

him." Anna stepped aside to let Emma come out, as well.

The girls looked at each other, then at him. "Where's Laura? I hope you're not too angry with her. She just wanted to help," Anna said.

"We did tell her not to," Emma added.

He didn't fault the girls at all for Laura's actions. She'd made the decision on her own.

"You're not in trouble," he said, smiling at them.

"But is she? Don't be mad, Papa."

Anna didn't usually take to most people, but here she was, defending Laura, even though she had no idea what had gone on. Owen still wasn't sure how he was going to tell the girls about Lena's injuries. How did one explain a gunshot wound to children?

"Promise us you're not mad," Emma said.

Owen took a deep breath. He tried not to lie to them, which was why coming up with an explanation was hard enough. But to promise something when every bone in his body was screaming in frustration with the woman...

"Girls—"

"Who's that coming?" Anna asked, pointing behind Owen.

Automatically, Owen put his hand on his gun belt as he turned. Then he relaxed.

"It's Uncle Will."

"Do you think he brought everyone with him? That's a lot of horses," Emma said.

Once again, he was going to have to disappoint the girls.

"I'm afraid not."

"You have to go to work again, don't you, Papa?" Anna's voice was tinged with sadness. When they'd moved to the ranch, it was with the promise that he wouldn't be gone for days on end anymore. That he was going to remain here with them.

Today wasn't just the day when his barn was damaged and his sister was shot, it was also the day his promise to his daughters would be broken.

Hopefully, Will would have some good advice. It seemed like everything Owen had been doing was all wrong, and he didn't know how to make it right again.

The girls ran ahead to greet Will, and Owen followed, still carrying the rooster. When Will saw him, he'd probably think he'd lost it, but there was something oddly comforting about stroking the soft feathers of an animal who'd once been the family nemesis but was now the family pet.

The yard was filling up with riders, and Owen was grateful for all of them, even if they hadn't gotten here in time to be much help. He spied Richard McDonald, one of the men who worked at the Leadville Fire Department. After nodding at Will, Owen continued to Richard.

"We had a small barn fire. I think it's out, but I'd appreciate it if you'd take a look."

"Sure thing." Richard dismounted and handed his reins to another member of the posse then followed Owen to the barn.

Laura sat on a stool, staring at the charred bits like she thought they were going to jump up and bite her.

"You can go on into the house now. Richard will take it from here."

Her jerky nod told him that she was still upset over everything that had happened. She probably thought he'd been too harsh with her, and maybe she was right. But thanks to her, his sister had been shot, the barn had nearly burned down and James had gotten away. He supposed he had the right to hang on to his anger for a while longer.

Owen took a deep breath and reminded himself of God's mercy, and how God forgave him all the stupid things he'd done over the years, so he needed to extend that mercy to Laura. But it didn't keep his insides from burning.

But there were more important things to worry about right now than the morality of his anger.

"On your way, would you ask Will about a doctor and see if he's got someone who can check Lena's wound? Then show them to the girls' room?"

Her expression softened at his request. "Of course."

Without any other comment, Laura got up and did as he'd asked. Or at least he assumed that's what she was doing.

After giving Richard a brief explanation of what happened, Owen exited the barn, just as Will was arriving.

"What happened here? Laura said Lena got shot."

Owen nodded. "Did you happen to have a doctor with you?"

"No, but I'd trust Jake with a bullet wound more than I'd trust half the doctors in town."

He knew Jake. Jake had pulled a bullet out of him once and had done the best job of it. A man shouldn't have multiple experiences getting bullets taken out him, but at least Owen had always been on the right side of the law.

"Me, too," Owen said.

Will gave him a strange look. "Can we start with the rooster? I don't think I've ever seen a man carrying around a rooster like it was a baby."

He hadn't even realized he was still carrying the animal. Owen set the rooster down, but it continued following him. Even though it couldn't possibly have known what it had done, the rooster seemed to have formed an attachment to Owen.

So Owen launched into the tale, knowing that all the men would have a good laugh at the idea of a life-saving rooster. He also had to include Lena's crazy horse in the life-saving category, something she'd probably hold over his head for the rest of his life.

But he'd take the teasing if it meant having his sister around awhile longer, a lot longer.

A scream came from inside the house, and Owen and the men all ran in the direction of it. It was Anna or Emma, he couldn't tell. But it felt like he was wading upstream trying to get to them, even though it had probably taken less than a minute.

The girls were standing in the kitchen, where Lena's blood was all over the place. A bloodied rag sat on the table, and in the eyes of two little girls, it was a frightening sight. Owen was a grown man and even he wanted to be sick. But mostly, that was because he knew whose blood it was, and it was a reminder of how close he'd come to losing Lena.

A breathless Laura entered the kitchen. "Are you all right?"

His daughters just stood there, holding each other, not saying a word.

Laura went to them. "I'm so sorry about the mess. Your aunt hurt her leg, and I got carried away trying to help her and I didn't get a chance to clean up. You remember what it was like with Henry's leg."

At the mention of the rooster, the girls relaxed.

"Where is Auntie?" Anna asked.

Emma nodded, and Owen noticed that she looked to Laura, not him. His girls had taken a shine to Laura, as evidenced by the way they'd defended her earlier and looked to her now. Did Laura understand how rare that was?

"She's upstairs," Laura said. "She's got someone who knows leg injuries better than me looking at it right now, but we can go see her in a while. Why don't we go into the library and make her a nice get-well card?"

And just like that, Laura had taken care of the problem of helping his daughters understand what had happened while they were in the root cellar. At some point, they'd want to know how Lena had hurt her leg, but at least now, they were reassured and happy.

"She's good with them," Will said.

Owen let go a little of the anger he felt toward Laura. "She is."

"You know, it's none of my business, but—"

With a glare at his old friend, Owen said, "When you start a sentence with it being none of your business, that's where it stops. What's most important right now is that we figure out a new plan for catching James and keeping Laura and my family safe."

As Will nodded in agreement, Owen realized there was one part of the plan he hadn't considered. His girls were becoming attached to Laura. How would he keep their hearts safe once he was done protecting her?

He'd already figured on his heart getting broken, but it didn't seem right to involve his daughters, as well.

Chapter Ten

Laura managed to keep the girls busy in the library while she set the kitchen to rights. She'd made a big mess of things, but at least this disaster was one she could easily fix.

She grabbed the bucket to go out to the well, and when she opened the back door, she saw the rooster sitting there, as though he was expecting to be let in.

"Did you want to come inside? I have to get some water first, then we'll help you out, all right?"

The rooster cocked his head as though he understood exactly what she was saying. Then he followed her to the well, where he seemed to wait patiently while she drew the water. Clearly she was crazy for giving a rooster such human attributes, but after today, Laura couldn't say she was sure of her sanity anymore anyway.

Once she got the water, she turned to go back to the house, and the rooster followed. Silly bird.

She set the bucket on the table then glanced at

Henry. He wasn't wearing the contraption to prevent him from making a mess all over the floor. She wasn't going to scrub the kitchen only to have to redo everything to get rid of rooster droppings.

"Hi, Henry," Laura said, bending down to the bird. "Do you think I could pick you up? Would that be all right?"

Though she'd seen everyone else carrying the rooster around, she'd never even touched the creature. Henry looked at her like he thought she was crazy. She probably was.

She bent and gently picked him up, trying to remember how she'd seen the girls do it. And, just as she'd observed with Owen carrying Henry around, she tucked him into her arm like a baby. The rooster seemed content with this arrangement, so Laura carried him into the library.

"Hello, girls." Laura smiled at them. "Henry wanted to come inside, but he's not wearing his um, covering, and I don't want him to make a mess."

The girls giggled as she stumbled over the word, *covering*, then Anna smiled at her.

"We can help you. You have to do it a special way so that you don't hurt him," she said, reaching for the rooster.

Though everyone had said Anna was the shy one of the twins, Laura had noticed the opposite. Where Emma barely spoke to her at all, Anna seemed to have taken to Laura. Which was so frustrating, considering the fact that Laura had been telling herself not to get attached.

It seemed so unfair that the girls' natural mother had thrown them away when Laura would have given anything to realize her dream of having children. She almost hated knowing the story, even though it had given her a lot of answers about the family.

Someone had suggested that Laura adopt a child from an orphanage, but no one would give a woman on her own a chance. People wanted a family for a child, not a divorced woman with a scandalous past. The scandal wasn't even her own doing, but it didn't matter. People still saw her as the murderer's wife.

With a sigh, she turned her attention back to the girls. Emma had taken out a bonnet and was spreading it on a table as Anna set the rooster on top of it.

"Now," Anna said. "You must be very gentle with Henry when you do this. He is very del-i-cate, and you don't want to hurt him."

Once again, Laura was struck by how much the children had picked up from their father and Lena. Though Owen's heavy-handed ways irritated her, she couldn't find fault with him as a father. He was so good with the girls, so patient. More importantly, he did so much to empower them.

Laura's father would never have given Laura this kind of freedom or allowed her to do so much for herself. Why would she need to know how to do anything on her own? The expectation for most women was that they would find a good man to marry, and he would take care of everything for her. The trouble was, no one had prepared her for being married to a man who wasn't so good. Even if her parents had fostered the kind of closeness Owen had with his daughters, they'd been gone for some time now and couldn't advise her on anything.

And so, here she was, still learning basic life skills that no one had thought to teach her because a young lady of standing wasn't supposed to need to know these things. She supposed, even though being here at the ranch was proving to be an incredibly painful experience, she was learning valuable lessons about life on her own.

Once she could finally go home, she would take inventory of all the skills a woman on her own needed to know and come up with lessons to teach the women who came to her boardinghouse. Some had family to fall back on, but so many were forced to start new lives alone. Most lived in the hope of finding another man to take care of them.

But would the new man? What if he, too, was a bad man?

Anna cleared her throat. "Now, Laura, you must pay close attention to this part. Papa says that if you aren't careful, you could make it hard for the rooster to breathe."

"We wouldn't want that," Laura said, smiling at the little girl.

Owen was raising his girls to be confident, independent women who could do anything. They weren't going to need to find someone who could take care of them. No wonder Lena hadn't married. She didn't need a husband for all the things most women did.

As Anna demonstrated how to properly attire the

rooster, Laura couldn't help but smile. At six, the girls had far more skills than Laura did, and while it was humbling to be taught by a child, she loved seeing how the twins seemed to gain confidence as they shared their knowledge with someone else.

When Anna finished getting the rooster situated, she undid the covering and handed the animal to Laura. "Now it's your turn. Papa says that if you want to learn, you have to watch, and then you have to do it yourself."

Funny, that's exactly how Owen had been teaching her. Except, of course, when he'd gotten exasperated with her. He'd been angry today, accusing her of not trusting him. And worse.

Did she think he'd ever raise a hand to her?

In the sanity of a calm moment, no. She couldn't see him ever being violent. But sometimes, like this afternoon...

Was it her own fears? Or was it something in Owen? She'd failed to see James's dark side until it was too late.

Such thoughts were not productive. Laura turned her attention back to the rooster and followed Anna's directions as she got all the necessary parts covered.

"You did it!" Both girls cheered as she held up a properly attired rooster.

Henry gave a squak and started to flap his wings.

"He doesn't like having to be still for so long," Anna said. "You should let him go."

Laura did as she asked, and was rewarded with an approving smile.

"We like you, Laura," Anna said. "Emma and I think you should stay with us forever."

Laura's heart twisted at the words. "I can't."

"Yes, you can. There's plenty of room for you. You just have to tell Papa you're sorry for making him mad today. If he sends you to bed without supper, we'll save you some of ours and bring it to you when Papa goes out to feed the animals," Anna said.

Emma nodded. "We do it all the time."

Was it wrong to laugh at two little girls who came up with clever plans for evading their punishments?

"I wouldn't feel right doing that," Laura said instead. "If you're being punished, you should accept your punishment with dignity and grace. If he sends me to bed without supper, then I'll be getting what I deserve."

The girls looked at each other, then Anna turned to Laura. "But what if Papa sends you away? We heard him tell Uncle Will that you were making him crazy, and something had to be done. We don't want you to go away. You've got to make Papa understand that you're sorry and you'll never make him crazy again."

If only it were all as simple as that.

Knowing that Owen wanted to be rid of her put an unfamiliar ache in her heart. She'd heard from James often enough that she was a useless woman who didn't deserve to be alive. Those taunts had ceased hurting her a long time ago. But to know Owen didn't want her?

A heaviness settled in the pit of Laura's stomach. Leaving the girls was going to be hard. Maybe it would be best if Owen did send her away now before they all got too attached.

Owen entered the room, hat in hand. "Laura, may I speak with you privately for a moment?"

She took a deep breath. Even knowing what he was going to say wouldn't make this conversation easier. Especially since the girls looked at her so pleadingly, like they were counting on her to make things right with their father so she could stay. How she hated breaking the hearts of two sweet little girls. But what other choice did she have?

"Of course." Laura swallowed the lump in her throat and followed Owen out of the library and into his private study. He closed the door behind them and gestured to one of the chairs.

Laura looked around, having not been in this room before. It was decorated much like the library, lined with walls of books. However, a rather large desk dominated the room, and there were only two chairs for sitting. One more side of Owen that Laura had never seen before. But, she supposed, it made sense that as a rancher, he would also have a business side.

"I…" Owen shifted uneasily on his feet. "I was hard on you earlier," he said finally. "I let my temper get the best of me, and I spoke in haste. I apologize."

Laura took a deep breath. She hadn't liked how he'd spoken to her, but the things he'd said were true. "I accept your apology. But you only spoke the truth. I should have stayed in the root cellar as you asked. I'm sorry for the trouble I caused."

Nodding slowly, Owen turned to the window and

looked out. Laura could see the men walking around as if they were searching for clues.

"Still," he said. "I should have been kinder in my approach. It was wrong of me to blame you. There are a million things that could have been done differently by all of us. The important thing is that Lena is going to be all right. So now we have to focus on the plan for the future."

When he finally turned around, Laura could see the newly formed lines on his face. Even though he'd apologized, she couldn't help but wonder if he did still blame her. Despite his explanation, she continued to blame herself.

As much as she wanted to hold Owen's treatment of her against him, she was finding it hard to do so. It had been easy to compare him to James, but James had never apologized to her. He'd never taken responsibility for his actions the way Owen just had.

In the barn, Owen had told her that he wasn't James and that Laura couldn't compare him to her ex-husband. Perhaps, as much as she felt Owen had been unfair to her, she'd been unfair to him.

But where was the line between opening her heart to Owen and seeing him differently, and thinking their relationship was more than what it was? Even though he seemed perfectly able to separate his personal life and work, Laura didn't have that ability. The trouble with letting her anger at Owen go was that it was the only thing keeping her from believing their relationship could be something more.

Laura closed her eyes, remembering her conversation with God in the barn. She had to find a way to trust in the Lord, and that whatever His plan was for this situation, in the end, it would be all right. Holding grudges against people wasn't the way of the Lord, no matter what the excuse.

Help me, Lord.

It was all she knew to say, the way her heart was jumbled.

And while this conversation wasn't about Owen sending her away, somehow that would have almost seemed kinder, because now she'd have to do the hard work of following God's will and not her own.

Owen watched the emotions play on Laura's face. Had he hurt her irreparably? He'd known, when they were in the barn, that he'd been too hard on her. But Lena…

He glanced up at the ceiling. She was in bed just above them. Lena had been there for him at every stage of his life. The thought of losing her had been almost too much to bear. But as he'd seen the pain in Laura's eyes, that, too, seemed almost unbearable. This poor woman had been through so much already. How could he have added more hurt to the weight she already carried?

The worst part of it was, as he told Will what had happened, Owen had realized that while, yes, Laura had been the one to leave the safety of the root cellar, he'd been far too focused on her to notice that James had come far enough out of his hiding spot to be able to shoot at the women. Had Owen seen him then, he would have been able to get him, and this whole ordeal would be over.

But he'd been so worried about Laura that he'd lost sight of James for just enough time that the man had been able to shoot his sister.

That was why, as much as Owen wanted to give a better apology, a better explanation so that things could be all right between them again, he couldn't. He'd let her too far into his heart and cared too deeply for her. The wounded expression on her face when he'd chastised her mattered to him, and that put them all at risk.

And yet, he needed to find a way to distance himself from her while still doing his job. Especially given what he was about to ask her.

"Will says we need to go back to town. At least there we'll have enough men to take turns watching out for James."

Laura nodded slowly like she was expecting this outcome. But the next part... Owen took a deep breath. Was it too much to ask?

"I can't leave Lena and the girls here by themselves. Lena isn't going to be able to put any weight on her leg for a while, and if James comes back, I don't want her to have to face him alone. I was wondering if we could all stay at your boardinghouse together until James is apprehended."

She looked at him as though he spoke a foreign language. And maybe he did, but there was still more to what he needed from her.

"I know it's a lot to ask, but I'd need your help

taking care of Lena and the girls. Lena needs to stay in bed, and I'll be busy with the investigation. My daughters seem to have taken a shine to you, so I don't think they'll be much trouble. Will would let them stay at his house, but his wife is expecting again, and—"

"I'll do it," Laura said, straightening so that she looked like the heiress she was. "Lena was injured protecting me. It's only right that I assist in her recovery."

Owen took a deep breath. While Laura's agreement was exactly what he'd hoped to hear, he didn't want it to be borne of her guilt.

"Her injury isn't your fault," Owen said quietly. "I don't want you to do this because you feel guilty over what happened. Even if you hadn't appeared, she still could have been shot."

Will had pointed that out to him, reminding him that as simple as the situation with James had looked, any number of things could have gone wrong. Even so, Owen knew that the responsibility for the situation was on his head. Lena had been shot because Owen was paying too much attention to Laura. James had gotten away because Owen had chosen to keep his barn from burning down instead of chasing after him. Which, Will had firmly said, was the right decision. If the barn fire had gotten out of control, it could have started a grass fire, which could have turned into a forest fire and threatened many of the other ranches in the area.

But watching the way Laura shifted her weight, he wasn't sure she believed him.

Convincing her, however, meant exposing the deeper fears within. Things he hadn't even told Will, let alone admitted out loud. His last case before hanging up his badge, he'd made a mistake. He had been guarding a house with a woman and her children inside, and a lady in a carriage stopped to ask him directions. He took his attention off the house for only a moment, but in that time, the lady, who turned out to be in league with the criminal he was trying to stop, had hit him over the head and rendered him unconscious long enough to put the family in danger. While everything had turned out all right in the end, Owen still couldn't shake the guilt over how it had nearly ended.

He'd lost his edge.

And now with Laura in the picture, he had one more thing to distract him from his job.

Owen was the wrong man for the case, and with everything that had gone wrong today, they should have found someone else. But nothing he told Will about what happened in the barn with James had convinced the other man that Owen was unfit.

And here was this woman, whose wounded gaze made him feel even more inept.

"I'll do my best to follow your directions in the future," Laura said quietly.

How was he supposed to answer that? Yes, he wanted her compliance, but this seemed like such an empty victory. At what cost had her cooperation come?

But that didn't matter. Not if he wanted to keep his

focus on keeping them all alive. Instead, he changed the subject.

"I hope it's not too much of an inconvenience for us to stay at the boardinghouse. Mary, Will's wife, says there haven't been any guests since you left. I'm willing to pay what you think is right."

Laura shook her head. "I don't need your money. Putting James back behind bars will be payment enough."

He supposed she didn't need his money. After all, Laura was a woman of means. It just felt wrong to take advantage of her hospitality.

Especially when it was clear he'd wounded her so deeply. Worse, they were putting her out because Owen hadn't done his job properly in the first place.

Part of him wanted to do whatever it took to make things right with her, to bring the smile back to her face. But what good would that do him? Or her, for that matter? Fixing a relationship that wasn't real had no purpose but to hurt both of them in the end. Especially when navigating that relationship would take too much of his energy away from keeping them all safe.

He just didn't know how to protect his daughters' hearts. Having Laura care for them seemed to be the worst solution when they would all go back to their old lives soon enough. And Laura would no longer be part of their lives.

Suddenly the easy solution seemed even more complicated.

"Very well," Owen said. For now, he'd let the matter drop. Maybe it was better this way, going back to the initial awkwardness that had been between them when she first came to the ranch.

The door opened, and Will walked in, confirming Owen's decision to let things drop. They didn't need an audience for their conversation.

"We need to get moving. The men confirmed that James hid in the wagon before making his move. I suspect he arrived sometime in the night, which is why you didn't see him coming. It looks like he made himself a makeshift bed in there and slept."

Owen had already come to the same conclusion. "Why did he wait so long? We were out in the yard all morning with the horses. He could have easily picked us off."

"I'm guessing he was passed-out drunk. There was an empty liquor bottle in there, and I know you don't drink."

Laura had stood to join them. "But how did he get here?"

"We saw a loose horse on our way here. He probably rode partway, then abandoned it to come the rest of the way on foot. From what I understand, the description of the horse matches one that was stolen in town a couple of days ago. Some of the deputies have gone to catch it just in case."

"How did he figure out we were here so quickly?" Owen asked.

Will's brows furrowed. "Only a handful of men knew the plan. If the horse is the same one that was stolen, that means James knew you'd gone to the ranch within hours of your leaving town."

The look Laura gave Will made even Owen's palms sweat. "If you knew a horse was stolen, why didn't you assume it was James and take action?"

Will gave her the patient smile he gave people when they asked an ignorant question. Sometimes Owen wished he'd developed that skill. He could certainly use it in most of his conversations with Laura.

"Do you know how many horses are reported stolen each day?"

Laura gave him a blank look. Owen tried not to chuckle. When he'd been assigned to investigate stolen horses, they got dozens each day. In a town as large as Leadville, it wasn't surprising, considering the number of unsavory characters attracted to the saloons and houses of ill repute.

"Enough that we couldn't use it as credible evidence that James had arrived in Leadville. We had people all over the state looking for him, and this is the first confirmed sighting." Will didn't bother hiding his disgust as he spoke.

Owen could understand. Based on their previous conversation, Will suspected that someone within their department had been in contact with James and was feeding him information. But who? It sickened Owen to think that one of their own was betraying them. He and Will had both thought they knew the men in the Sheriff's Office.

They'd been wrong.

And that hurt almost as much as nearly losing his

sister. Men he trusted, had fought beside, risked his life with... How could someone they knew so well turn against them?

"I'm sure he has enough people who owe him favors that he's going to be impossible to find," Laura said.

Owen shook his head. "I don't believe in impossible. I'll admit that this adds a degree of difficulty, but we've faced worse before."

They'd never faced having a traitor in their midst. But at least, moving forward, Owen had Will to back him up. Will was the finest lawman he knew, and with Will on their side, they were sure to get James in the end.

"True," Will said, then he turned to Laura. "Owen refuses to take credit for it, but he is the reason we were able to bring down the Hart Brothers."

Owen hated it when people brought up that case. It was merely a coincidence that had led the law to the hideout. All right, it was more than a coincidence. Owen had seen his wayward wife riding out of town, and he'd gone after her to try to talk sense into her. He'd heard rumors that she was keeping company with Buddy Hart and was thinking to warn her. He'd ended up making the greatest arrest of his career. But everyone thought he was a hero.

He wasn't a hero. Just a confused husband.

Sadie had told him that being an outlaw's mistress was more fun than being a lawman's wife. She'd started bragging about all the exciting things she'd done with Buddy, and Buddy, not wanting her to incriminate him further, had pulled out his gun and killed her.

Had the posse not seen Owen riding out, the story would have had a different ending. But they hadn't been too far behind and arrived just in time.

No great lawman skill there, just a lot of coincidence.

But he couldn't say that without telling Laura the whole story about Sadie. He'd already shared too many personal details with her. Why had he told her so much about his family?

One more reason it was best to have this distance between them. He'd done the right thing by apologizing to her, and she'd done the right thing by accepting it. Even though they both knew that none of those words had been adequate in resolving Laura's hurt feelings.

It just seemed as though sharing anything with Laura would only serve to complicate an already muddy mess.

"Enough of all this talk," Owen said. "I need to get some things packed for the girls, and I imagine Laura needs to pack, as well."

He turned back to Laura. "How much time do you need to be ready to go?"

"Only a few minutes. I didn't bring much, as you may recall."

Her words had an icy quality to them, and they stung more than they should have. The trouble with doing the right thing for them long-term meant a painful short term.

"Good." He turned to Will. "Do you think the wagon is safe to take to town? Lena won't be able to ride."

Will nodded. "The men are checking it out as we speak."

But was there, among those men, someone who'd betrayed them?

"I'd like for the two of us to take a second look. I thought I could trust every man we have, but clearly, we are going to have to be extra vigilant."

Will looked pained as he nodded. Probably because while Owen had hung up his badge, Will was still working to bring justice to the people of Leadville. Not knowing who he could trust put all of their cases in jeopardy.

Even though they were supposed to be protecting Laura, the stakes were even higher if they didn't figure out who was helping James. When a lawman was for sale, no one was safe.

Chapter Eleven

When they finally arrived at her boardinghouse, Laura was relieved to see that everything was as she'd left it. Mary came out the front door with her little girl on her hip, and the twins immediately jumped off the wagon.

"Aunt Mary! Rosabelle!"

Owen turned and smiled at Laura. "She's not their real aunt, in case you were wondering. But our families have always been close, and we love them like family."

"Mary is a friend of mine, as well," Laura said, smiling at him. "I'm glad we share the connection."

Though she hadn't needed Owen's explanation about Mary, it felt good that he was trying to establish a semblance of normalcy between them despite their earlier quarrel. Of course, calling it a quarrel seemed to diminish what had happened.

But that small bit of conversation was all she was going to get out of Owen right now. He gave a quick nod, then turned to give instructions to one of the deputies who'd ridden alongside their wagon on the way to town.

He blamed her for Lena's injury. True, he'd apologized for his words and had even tried to explain why he was wrong and that it wasn't her fault. But while he said all the right things, there had been something in his demeanor lacking sincerity. Like he'd been holding back what he really thought.

As much as Laura wanted to hold it against him, how could she? Owen was right. Even if what Owen said was true, and Lena's injury could have happened at any point in the situation with James, the fact was, it had been Laura's mistake that had gotten Lena out of the house and into the line of fire.

The only reason Laura could even hold her head up was that Lena, who'd ridden on a pallet in the wagon, was going to be all right. One of the men had given her something to help the pain that also made her sleep most of the journey. Laura had ridden the entire way sitting next to Lena, watching over her, and praying that the other woman would have no lasting ill effects from her injury.

As if she knew Laura was thinking about her, Lena murmured something incoherent in her sleep. Owen came back around the side of the wagon.

"I've got some men to help me carry Lena in, and the doctor is on his way. If you would be so good as to show me to the room you'd like Lena to stay in, that would be appreciated."

Laura stood and brushed the hay off her dress as

she took Owen's hand to be helped out of the wagon. The electric shock she'd once felt in his touch was almost like a sting. Reminding her that everything she had been attracted to in him was an illusion. Why would she even want a man who thought so little of her?

Taking a deep breath, Laura strengthened her resolve to not view Owen as anything more than a lawman doing his job. Why would she even like someone who'd hurt her feelings so deeply? Why did she care so much about what Owen thought?

But then he smiled at the girls, who were holding hands with Rosabelle and playing Ring Around the Rosie. Anyone could tell his daughters were the center of his existence, and such tenderness and love couldn't be ignored. How could she be angry with a man who hadn't lashed out at her in meanness and cruelty, but out of the pain of seeing a beloved family member almost die?

Was it too much to want that kind of love for herself?

Perhaps it wasn't just about Owen. She watched Will greet his wife with a tender kiss as he patted her slightly rounded stomach, and the twinge of envy Laura felt wasn't wholly unexpected. All she'd ever wanted was the love of a good man and a family of her own. What she'd gotten was a divorce from an evil man and no hope of ever having children. She knew the Lord had plans she didn't understand, but sometimes, they seemed incredibly unfair.

Laura followed Owen into the house. He paused at

the stairs, but Laura gestured toward the back of the house. "I know Lena isn't able to stand right now, but I believe it will be easier if she takes my room. That way, help is close at hand, and when she can walk, she won't have to manage the stairs."

He hesitated like he was going to argue with her, but then he nodded. "As long as it doesn't put you out."

"Not at all. The other rooms are quite pleasant, and I will sleep better knowing that Lena won't have to worry about the stairs."

She led Owen to her room, grateful that she'd tidied it up before they left. Not that she was messy, and he'd already seen it, considering the way he'd hovered over her while she packed. But she hadn't been thinking beyond her anger at being forced to do something she didn't want to do when he'd last been here. Now, she was aware of how he took in the room, his glance sweeping over her neatly made bed, covered by a quilt the ladies at church had made her, her mother's bureau, which she'd brought from Denver, and the small bedside table that held a lamp that she'd thought too pretty to resist. What did he think of her room? Did he think it as impractical as he'd found her parlor? Was it another blemish on her character?

Shoving those thoughts out of her mind, Laura smiled at him as she said, "I'm sure Lena will find it comfortable in here."

A group of men entered the house with the bed contraption they'd created to carry Lena. Owen had called it something, but Laura couldn't remember. She supposed it didn't matter.

"In here, please," Laura said, going around the side of the bed to pull back the covers. She'd changed her sheets when she'd done the others the day they'd left, so everything was acceptable for a guest.

At least in that, no one could fault her.

Laura stepped out of the way as the men brought Lena in. Lena smiled weakly at her, and her expression was almost vacant. Definitely not herself. Laura said a quick, silent prayer that Lena would find relief from her pain soon.

The men put Lena on the bed, then left the room.

"Thank you," Laura said to the departing men, then turned to Lena. "Are you comfortable enough? I can bring more pillows, more blankets, anything you need."

Lena's eyes fluttered closed, then back open again. "No fussing. I'll be fine. Don't let that brother of mine bully you into thinking you have to wait on me. No matter what anyone says, this isn't your fault."

Her last words seemed to take forever for her to get out, and as she spoke, her eyes drifted closed again. Moments after she said her piece, a tiny snore escaped her mouth.

"I suppose we should let her rest," Laura said, looking at Owen. His expression betrayed nothing about what he'd thought of Lena's speech, but that was probably for the best. She couldn't handle any more guilt.

He nodded. "The doctor should be here soon. In

the meantime, why don't you show me where you'd like the rest of us?"

As she passed by him to exit the room, Owen took her by the arm. "And she's right. I already apologized for what I said, but I hope you know that you don't have to put yourself out or go to extreme measures to ease your conscience. I want to inconvenience you as little as possible."

His touch was gentle but firm. James used to delight in jerking her by the elbow, sometimes sending her flying across the room. But there was no violence in Owen, and his eyes were filled with kindness and sympathy. She'd never seen that in James. Not even when they were courting. Back then, she'd thought his eyes mysterious, though now she recognized that they were shifty. But there was no mistaking the gentleness in Owen's expression.

Considering Owen's words, Laura took a deep breath. Perhaps she was wrong to mistrust his apology. James and his false non-apologies had hardened her heart to the genuine sincerity of others. It had taken Laura months to accept the friendship of the ladies in the Leadville community because she'd been worried about their motives.

Maybe she needed to start trusting Owen, as well.

"I'm not helping Lena out of guilt," Laura said. "She was kind to me in your home and provided for my comfort. I will do no less for her. This is how I treat all my guests."

Owen hesitated, and in that hesitation, Laura realized that they both had a lot of work to do in the trust department. Though Laura had thought she trusted Owen, and perhaps, the first time around, she had. But somehow, in establishing her independence, she'd become so desperate to prove it that she'd lost her ability to believe in other people's judgment. Here was Owen, needing to give her that same trust, and he was struggling against his self-reliance and with letting Laura lead.

Or at least that's how it seemed to Laura.

Something in that realization gave her hope. And courage. He was struggling just as much as she was to adjust to the situation. A thought that gave her a great deal of compassion for the man standing before her.

Laura led him up the stairs and stopped on the landing. "There are three bedrooms up here, all of which are equally comfortable. But I'll let you choose which one you feel is most advantageous for you to do your job."

His shoulders relaxed slightly. "You don't mind if I look around?"

"I would be pleased if you did. Our primary concern right now is safety, and I believe you would know best how to handle it."

Did he see the olive branch she was extending? Telling him that she was going to let him do what he felt best and she would abide by that decision?

Owen said nothing as he walked into the first bedroom, a rather feminine room adorned with all sorts of lace that had seemed like a good idea at the time. James used to mock Laura for her love of beautiful things, and as a result, her surroundings had been more masculine than she would have liked. When Laura came up with her boardinghouse idea, she'd hoped to create places that were a haven for women. She hadn't thought that she'd ever have a man as a guest.

He went through the next two rooms, going straight to the windows and peering out. Of course, he didn't notice the decor. Once again, Laura was being silly in even worrying that he might find the rooms objectionable in that way. Owen's only concern was the safety of the room. A fact brought home to her when she watched him try every window.

All locked, which Laura hadn't remembered doing. When Owen arrived the other day, she'd had them all open to air the space out. And, for the first time, Laura realized the rooms were now a bit stuffy again.

"We can open the windows if you like," Laura said, stepping into the room Owen now occupied.

"No. I had Will make sure they were secured when we left. All James needs is an opening, and everyone is at risk. I realize it will be uncomfortable, but for now, you must leave all the windows closed and locked."

He looked at her like he didn't trust her to listen. She was starting to hate that expression, and yet, she deserved it.

"Of course," Laura said. "I understand completely. Do you have a preference for where everyone will stay?"

"I'll take this one. If I were breaking into a home, this is the entry I'd use. You'll sleep in the front bedroom, because it's in the open, and anyone would be stupid to try to access it with that many men guarding the area. The girls can share the other one."

It wasn't much of an explanation, but it was more than Owen had ever given her at her first question. Could he also be learning to compromise in their rocky relationship?

"That sounds fine. Thank you for sharing your thoughts with me."

He gave her a strange look, but Laura hoped that if she affirmed the actions that made her feel good, he'd continue to act accordingly. She'd hated his lack of communication, so she would do her best to acknowledge when he did tell her things. Hadn't she heard Pastor Lassiter say something about that in church? Focusing on the bad only brought more bad, but when you focused on the good, you would get more of it.

"Would you mind getting the girls settled in? I want to discuss our next steps with Will. I'd also like to see if the doctor has arrived yet."

Owen didn't wait for an answer as he went back down the stairs.

She supposed there wasn't much else to talk about, but even with the strides they'd made in their relationship, it seemed more strained than ever. Once again, Laura had to question her interpretation of the situation. Was Owen being distant, or was he just trying to do his job? Or was it both?

Sighing, Laura went downstairs to look for the girls. They were in the parlor, showing Rosabelle their dolls. Mary sat on the couch, watching them with a doting expression on her face.

"They seem to adore having a little one to play with," Laura said, entering the room.

Mary smiled. "They do. Will keeps telling Owen he should remarry to give the girls a sibling of their own, but Owen insists that the girls are all he needs. I know a lot of men want sons, but there's something special about the bond a father has with his daughters."

The other woman placed her hand on her stomach with such a satisfied look that Laura once again had to force herself not to be envious. "Will says he'd like another daughter," Mary continued. "But I know he will love a son just the same. What matters is having a happy, healthy baby, and even the happy doesn't matter so much."

Shaking her head, Mary gave a small chuckle. "You've met my nephew, Matthew. You didn't know him as a baby, but he was the most disagreeable infant anyone had ever seen. Most of the time, he was inconsolable, and yet, my sister Rose was so loving and patient with him. Now, of course, he is an absolute delight."

The warmth in Mary's voice wasn't meant to hurt Laura, and certainly Mary didn't know of Laura's private pain. Laura, too, would accept a disagreeable baby. An ill baby, if only to have a child of her own. Impossible.

Laura forced a smile as she gave a murmur of

agreement. It wasn't Mary's fault that Laura was miserable.

Anna looked up from her playtime with the others and smiled at Laura.

"Papa says we get to stay here at your house."

Anna got up and came to sit beside her. Big blue eyes that looked so much like her father's stared up at Laura. "You must be lonely living here all by yourself. I'm glad we can keep you company."

The little girl took Laura's hand, and Laura nearly wept from the innocent kindness the child offered. How could her mother have abandoned her and her sister? Once more, Laura was struck with deep admiration for Owen and Lena. Not just for taking care of the children, but for how they were raising two such thoughtful girls. It was hard to hold on to her prejudice against him when he clearly had enough goodness in him to raise such children.

But in a lot of ways, that only deepened Laura's confusion about the kind of man Owen Hamilton was. And what her feelings for him should be.

One of the men entered the room, holding a wicker basket at arm's length. The basket was rocking violently of its own accord. Or so it seemed.

"Ma'am? What am I supposed to do with this?"

The girls jumped up. "Henry!"

They ran to the basket, but the man held firm. "Owen says we were to ask you what to do with this so as not to cause you too much inconvenience."

"Well, let's put that poor creature out of his misery. He must be so uncomfortable in there." Laura took the basket from him, then turned to the girls. "You need to take the same care at my house as you did at yours with Henry. Any messes will be your responsibility, do you understand?"

Two blond heads nodded as Laura opened the basket. Henry flew out, squawking. The mess inside the basket was terrible. Laura turned to the man who'd brought the rooster in.

"I hate to trouble you, but this needs to be taken out and cleaned. Are we allowed to go outside to the yard to do it?"

He hesitated like he didn't know the answer, but Owen walked in. "Thanks, John. I'll take it from here."

Owen looked like he was about to say something, but then a crash from the other side of the room took Laura's attention away from him.

"Oh dear!" The rooster had flown into Laura's vase and sent it crashing to the floor. Then he'd spun in Rosabelle's direction. Though he didn't hit her or injure her, the little girl screamed and started to cry.

"I'll get him!" Emma chased after the bird from one direction, but her sister copied her actions, and within seconds, the two girls had bumped into each other, and the rooster was still on the loose.

Laura held out her arms, and that silly bird flew right into them as if that's what he'd intended all along.

The force of the landing caused Laura to stumble, but as she wrapped her arms around him, she regained her footing.

As Laura smoothed the rooster's wings into place, she noticed that her parlor was in shambles. Glass from the vase was everywhere, it seemed, and stray feathers were scattered here and there. Mary had taken her daughter into her arms and was comforting the little girl. When Laura turned back to the twins, they stared at her, wide-eyed.

"Please, Miss Laura, don't send Henry to the stew pot," Anna said, her lower lip trembling.

Emma nodded. "Please. He didn't mean to make such a mess."

The rooster cocked his head at her like he, too, was pleading for his life.

Laura closed her eyes and shook her head slowly. What kind of insanity had she embarked upon, worrying about the feelings of a rooster?

"I'm sorry. We'll pay for any damages. I just... after what he did, and with the way the girls begged, I couldn't leave him behind." Owen sounded truly sorrowful as he spoke. He, too, seemed unable to resist the rooster's charms.

Stroking the silky feathers that she'd found comfort in at the ranch, Laura opened her eyes and looked at them.

"There is no way I could ever eat this rooster. Or let anyone else, for that matter. However, I will hold you to your promise of cleaning the mess."

Then Laura looked around the room. "As for paying for damages, my parlor is highly unsuitable to have animals or children playing in it. I should have considered that sooner. Owen, you will take the children, the rooster and the basket outside to get that cleaned up. Mary, if you and Rosabelle could find me a box to put my breakable items in, I'll get those stored away so nothing else is damaged. I will find a broom so I can get the glass swept up. While it is the children's responsibility to clean up after themselves, in this case, it's best if an adult handles the glass."

Owen looked at her with an expression of…was that respect she saw gleaming in his eyes?

"That sounds like a good plan. There's an empty crate in the back of the wagon we can use for your things so Mary needn't trouble herself," Owen said.

Mary smiled, still rubbing her daughter's back. "I think Rosabelle is past due for her nap. You won't mind if I take her home, will you?"

"Not at all," Laura said. "I think we have things well in hand here, but I greatly appreciate your assistance."

Owen came over to Laura and took Henry out of her arms. "Come on, fella. Let's get some fresh air."

He and the girls left the room, and Mary stood, adjusting Rosabelle on her hip. "You're letting them keep a pet rooster? In your house?"

Laura sighed. Explaining the situation seemed to be far more effort than it was worth. Especially since Mary's little one was still fussing slightly. The child needed a nap, not another delay.

"It will be fine," Laura said instead.

As Mary passed her, she patted Laura gently on the arm. "I hope so. But since you have no children of your own, you may not realize that you don't always have to do what the children want. Saying yes at the time might keep them happy temporarily, but children also need to learn how to accept being told no gracefully."

The twist of Mary's words in Laura's heart was almost too painful to bear. Though she meant them without malice, particularly since Laura had not shared her deepest longing with the other woman, it was hard to hear the cold truth thrown in her face.

"Thank you," Laura said, trying to keep her voice steady.

"Of course." Mary smiled and gave her another pat on the arm. "I know you're not used to being around children, and with Owen busy and Lena incapacitated, I'm more than happy to help anytime. When they lived in town and Lena needed a break while Owen worked, I often looked after the girls. I know Will wants me to rest, but I feel terrible leaving you alone to such a task."

Laura took a deep breath. "I'll be fine. I frequently spend time with my friend Nellie Jeffries and her children, and I'm sure everything will work out."

Nodding, Mary said, "That's right. I'd forgotten you and Nellie were friends. Nellie is an excellent mother. I'm sure she'd be delighted to assist you, as well. You know her husband bought Owen's old house, right? Perhaps you could take the children for a visit if Owen thinks it safe. I'm sure the girls would love to see their former home."

Clearly Mary had no idea how hard Laura was struggling to keep her emotions in check. She spoke of mothering and visiting as though they were the same thing and easily accomplished. Even the casual mention of their friend Nellie was another knife in her heart. Nellie, too, was barren, but she'd managed to marry a man who had children and had become a mother to them.

Could Laura marry a man and care for his children? Perhaps, but she wasn't willing to do as Nellie had done and become a mail-order bride, marrying a man she barely knew. True, it had worked out for Nellie, but Laura wasn't so sure she could find happiness the same way. She'd thought she'd known James, and he'd turned out to be a monster. She'd thought she'd loved James. Big mistake. And then there was Owen, who she'd thought she had grown to care for, but she'd misinterpreted all of his actions.

How could she trust herself to know if she'd found love for real in the future?

Perhaps Nellie would be a good person to talk to. Mary seemed to lead such a charmed life, with a respectable family and a wonderful husband. Nellie at least knew what it was like to be married to a horrible man, then find love again.

"I'll discuss visiting Nellie with Owen. Now I insist you and Rosabelle go get some rest. I'd hate for Will to be cross with us all." Laura's smile hurt almost more than she could bear. But she couldn't let the other woman know how deeply wounded she was.

Fortunately, Mary didn't seem to notice as she shook her head. "He is so overprotective. But I love him, and I know he means well, so I'll do just that."

Was that what love was? Knowing the other person was being overprotective and overzealous but choosing to obey anyway? Like the girls in the root cellar, irritated with their father, but knowing his orders came from love. James used to tell Laura that her marriage vows said she must obey him no matter what, and though Laura had tried, she'd felt smothered and stifled by that command. Did true love take one to a place where obedience wasn't a chore? And would her childless state ever stop hurting?

As the door closed behind Mary, Laura sank into her favorite spot on the sofa and surveyed the room once more. The mess in what was once her refuge seemed to reflect the mess in her heart. And then, because she couldn't hold it in any longer, she began to sob.

The other men had found some rope to create another leash for the rooster, so it could roam around the bit of grass in Laura's backyard. With so many deputies in the area, Owen felt safe letting the girls play outside. Will hadn't had many men to spare, but as word spread among their acquaintances that Owen needed help, several men had volunteered to take turns guarding the family.

Owen bent to pick up the basket for the unpleasant task of cleaning it out, then realized he'd forgotten it in the parlor. He shook his head. It was good of Laura to be so accepting of the rooster, especially in light of the mess it had made. Lena would have thrown a fit if that thing had done that kind of damage in their house. The rooster would definitely have been back in the barnyard, if not on their supper table.

She might be a pampered city girl, but Owen appreciated how Laura was so quick to take to their ways and learn new things. He'd underestimated her.

When he got to the parlor, he saw Laura crying.

Owen squeezed his eyes shut. He should have known that everything was not as wonderful as it seemed. Why couldn't she have just told him to begin with? The sound of the girls' laughter hit his ears. Of course. She'd gone out of her way to be kind to his daughters. Whatever faults Laura had, he was willing to overlook them because of how good she was to his girls.

And he was going to have to eat his pride to make right whatever had this woman crying like her heart was breaking. She hadn't even cried like this through her first ordeal with James. She'd stoically accepted the situation, and the only deep emotion she'd shown was in the nightmares that terrorized her in her sleep.

He took a deep breath, entered the room and knelt before her. "I'm so sorry, Laura. Please don't cry."

Though it wasn't proper, he couldn't help but put his hands on her knees in a gesture of comfort.

She looked up at him, her face red with tears and pain. "I'll be fine. Please. I just need a moment."

"You don't have to pretend to be brave." He looked at her, hoping she understood the compassion he was offering her. "I wish I could take back the horrible things I said to you in the barn. James is out there trying to hurt you, and I lost control and hurt you with my words. I know we talked, and you forgave me, but clearly, you're deeply wounded."

Laura shook her head. "It's not that. Please. Leave me."

If not him, then… Owen looked around the room.

"I'm sorry about the rooster. I'll see if one of the men can take him for the time being. Surely someone has a shed or a chicken coop of their own."

"The rooster isn't a problem." Her whole body shuddered from the effort of taking a breath. "I… just…need…to be left alone."

More tears streamed down her face, and Owen couldn't help but take her in his arms. He'd seen many a sobbing woman before, but none had affected him so. All he wanted to do was hold Laura and make whatever it was that had her so upset better.

As he held her, she clung to him tighter, her tears soaking his shirt.

Was it wrong of him to think of how her hair smelled like sunshine? The sun would be going down soon, and the picnic they'd shared earlier in the day seemed like it had been weeks ago. How he wished he could change the events that had put a wedge between them.

"I'm not going to leave you," Owen whispered. "I'm here for you. I'll protect you."

He'd given her that promise of protection once before, which was why they were all here. But this wasn't about his duty to a badge he'd given up months ago. No, today's promise was something more.

Losing Sadie had been devastating. He'd given

her his heart, but in the end, it hadn't been enough. Yet as he held Laura, who'd been trying so hard to be strong in the face of so many difficulties, he couldn't justify withholding his heart any longer.

When she found her footing and no longer needed him, Laura would leave him just as Sadie had. Just as his mother had before her. But maybe that's who God created him to be. The man who gave his heart to save a woman who couldn't love him back. Somehow, in that, he had to trust that God knew what he was doing.

Laura's sobs had finally subsided. Owen stroked her hair, then pressed a quick kiss to the top her head. She looked up at him, then he got up and sat next to her on the sofa.

"Now," he said, "tell me what has you so upset."

"I'll never be a mother," she said slowly. "I'd accepted it, and I thought I could bear it, but it suddenly became too much. I don't begrudge Mary her happiness, but it's hard to see someone who has everything you ever wanted, and to hear her give advice because you're not a mother and she is."

Owen's chest tightened as he remembered how Laura's biggest emotional reaction to James's betrayal had been finding out that the reason he'd murdered his mistress was that she'd been carrying his child. On nights when she'd been most melancholy, she'd talked about how she'd wanted children, and that was a dream now denied her.

How could he have forgotten?

And how could he have been so insensitive as to ask her to spend time with his daughters?

"I'm sorry," Owen said, looking her in the eye. "I just realized how difficult it must be for you, with the girls and all that."

Laura nodded. "How could their mother have not wanted them?"

Tears began to flow again, and Owen held her tight. He'd asked himself that same question hundreds of times over the years, and he hated that he could not find a single reasonable answer in his heart.

"I would have given anything..." Then Laura closed her eyes again and lay her head on his chest as though she was exhausted from letting out all those pent-up emotions.

Why had he married and had children with a woman who'd never expressed such a deep desire to be a mother? If he could have chosen a mother for his daughters, it would have been someone like Laura. Not just because the thought of not being a mother brought her to such a state of despair. But because she treated his children with such care and love. It was a rare woman who would be so understanding about a rooster in the house. Especially a rooster who destroyed her parlor.

Though he wasn't one to be presumptuous when it came to understanding God's ways, Owen had to admit that, in this case, he wondered what God was thinking. How could a woman as wonderful as Laura be rendered childless? And one as thoughtless as Sadie have twins she didn't want? In his work,

Owen had come across countless children who'd been unwanted by mothers, fathers or relatives assigned to care for them in the absence of parents.

Why hadn't God seen fit to give those children to a woman like Laura?

Please, God. Give Laura the comfort only You can give. I know You are a loving God, but I can't see beyond Laura's pain and what seems to be an unjust situation.

Owen kissed the top of her head again and gave her a tight squeeze. Having her in his arms felt so right, even though he knew he had crossed a line by being too familiar with her.

"I wish I could…" Owen said, but found he didn't have the words to finish.

What did he wish? That he could be the man to give her children? Owen shook his head. Lena told him all the time that he should find a wife and have more children, but Owen truly thought his family was complete. Anna and Emma were enough for him. As for a wife…if Owen were to marry again, it would be to someone who he knew would love him under all circumstances, and not just until she felt safe again. He wanted a true partner in life, and even if sharing a tender moment with Laura put the thought in his head, it didn't make it the right thing for either of them.

Laura was fragile, too fragile to know her own heart. And Owen needed a woman who loved him because she loved him, not because he represented the security she thought she craved.

So many things in his heart, and yet none were appropriate to voice. In that, he could understand some of Laura's struggle—having to hold in her pain because it wouldn't be proper to express it.

Laura looked up at him. "It doesn't matter. I'm barren. I can't have children. It's been confirmed by a doctor."

The words were spoken with such certainty that Owen hurt for her. What was it like to know that your deepest desire would never happen?

"I'm sorry," Owen said, knowing he'd already said it multiple times, but he had no other words to express the deep sorrow he felt for Laura's predicament.

She gave him the kind of wry smile that he loved, not because it was pretty, but because it was the truest demonstration of her feelings that he saw from her. She was unhappy but desperately trying to come to terms with it and find a way to live her life anyway.

"It's not your fault. You didn't make me barren." Laura pulled away from him and straightened. "I shouldn't have come apart like that. I'm usually not so unstable."

She was worried about being unstable? Owen shook his head. "I can't pretend to know what you're going through. But I remember how hard it was, and still is when the girls experience things that normal children go through with their mothers. They went through a phase where they would call every woman they met Mama, hoping that someone would answer."

Taking a deep breath, Owen searched her dark eyes, hoping he wasn't yet again saying the wrong thing. "I wanted so badly to take that pain away from them, but I couldn't. Lena and I do our best, but in the end, all we can do is love them and be there for them when it hurts."

Laura took a deep breath and squared her shoulders like she always did when she was trying to be brave. Owen was starting to love that about her. No matter how hard things got, she did her best to move forward and carry on with grace and dignity.

"Thank you for being willing to comfort me. That means a lot. But you have your duties, and I have mine. We should get back to work."

The sudden change was almost chilling. As Laura stood, Owen looked up at her. "Did I say or do something wrong?"

"No." Laura shook her head. "But since I'm being honest about my feelings, I also want to say that when you protected me before, I'd thought we'd become friends. I confided in you like I just did now. The things I said to you were things I've never said to another person. But then you left me. We lived in the same town, and not once did you come to call or acknowledge that you'd been an important part of my life. Then I found out about your family, and all the other things you never told me while I shared deeply personal information about my life."

The sadness in her eyes was unmistakable, and Owen hated that once again, she pointed to the pain he'd caused her.

"I apologize that my emotions overcame me and that you felt compelled to comfort me. But please don't do it again. It's too confusing to my heart, thinking I have a friend, then finding out it's only part of your job. I have a hard enough time trusting my judgment as it is. I need you to be clearer in your role in the future."

How could he disagree? Hadn't he already chastised himself for crossing the line multiple times?

Owen nodded. "Of course. I didn't mean to distress you further. I'll leave you now and get back to what I need to do."

He stood, then went over to the rooster's basket and picked it up. They both wanted things from each other that neither was capable of delivering. Owen cared about Laura, always would. But she was right. They both needed to stop fooling themselves into thinking that they would have something that wasn't meant to be.

Chapter Twelve

The doctor had agreed that Lena's injuries were not life threatening, especially since they'd come to town and she was receiving treatment. Laura was grateful for such positive news, especially when she went into Lena's room the next morning to find Lena sitting up in bed.

"I wish I'd known you were awake, I'd have come in here sooner," Laura said, coming around to the windows. "Would you like me to open the curtains and let some light in?"

"Please. I'm dying in this dark place, being treated like an invalid. I know you meant well with all your broth and sick-people food yesterday, but could I please get some real food today?"

Laura had always liked Lena's plain speech. She couldn't help but smile at the other woman's frustration at being stuck in bed. If the shoe were on the other foot, Laura would feel the same way.

"Absolutely. The doctor said the pain medicine

would upset your stomach and not to overdo it on food, but I've always believed that people should listen to their bodies when they're ill."

Lena nodded. "I couldn't agree more. Which is why I find it ridiculous that I have to stay in bed. Just my leg is hurt, not the rest of my body."

With the curtains open, Laura could see that it was going to be a beautiful day. Though it wouldn't likely be safe for Lena to go outside, she saw no harm in helping Lena to the parlor, where she could at least be part of the activity of the day.

"Can you manage to dress on your own? I packed simple garments for you in case you felt well enough to be out of bed. I'll see if Owen can get some men to help carry you into the parlor."

Though Lena visibly tensed at the idea of being carried into the parlor, she seemed happy at Laura's offer. "That would be wonderful, thank you."

As Laura turned to leave, Lena stopped her. "But first, I want to talk to you about something."

Laura sighed. The guilt discussion again. She'd humor an injured woman, but this was starting to become an old topic.

"Of course. Anything." She smiled despite her annoyance.

"Do you care for my brother?"

Laura stared at her. Not the discussion she'd had in mind.

"I don't know how to answer that question," she finally said. "And I don't think this is an appropriate topic right now."

She and Owen had been cordial since their encounter yesterday evening, but Laura had tossed and turned all night at the memory of his arms around her and the gentle press of his lips to her head. She'd never known such a loving touch from a man. It wasn't what she'd expected—she was surprised she wished for more of it. She'd never understood the allure of being in a man's arms, but after feeling so safe in Owen's, it made sense.

But she also understood how easily a woman could get burned.

Did she appreciate his comfort? Yes. Did she love how he'd made her feel? Yes. At least until she'd realized that his feelings didn't match hers. No wonder so many women compromised themselves for a man. Not that Laura believed Owen would dishonor her in any way. True, it had been improper for him to hold her so, but there were no illicit intentions there, which was one of the things that made her like him all the more.

"He's trying hard not to fall in love with you," Lena said. "Sadie, his late wife, was a witness to a murder. A gang was trying to kill her so she wouldn't testify. Owen was assigned to protect her, then he fell in love with her. She said she loved him, too, so they got married. Only being married to a lawman wasn't as exciting as she'd thought it would be, so she left."

Laura stared at her blankly. Owen had told her most of this, minus the part about him trying not to fall in love with her. "I know."

"Do you?" Lena gave her a much harsher look than

Laura would have thought the situation warranted. "My brother's heart is in danger, and you treat it like I've just told you that we're out of sugar."

What was she supposed to say in response? Lena acted like she expected an answer, and Laura had none to give.

"I believe you're mistaken," Laura said quietly. "I'm nothing but a job to him. Owen and I have been down this road before. I read too much into his actions, and I'll not do it again. I know you mean well, but I can't see him appreciating your meddling in his affairs. And neither do I."

Lena gave a quick nod, like she understood, and Laura left to find Owen. As she walked into the kitchen, she nearly ran straight into him.

"Is everything all right? How's Lena?" His face was filled with concern.

"She's fine." Laura tried to smile, but she found that Lena's words had left her feeling more unsettled than she'd have thought. "Actually, better than fine. She'd like to have some help out to the parlor so that she can sit amid the activity."

Owen frowned. "The doctor wanted her to rest."

"You know she'll go mad sitting in there by herself with nothing to do."

"True." Owen looked at her like he'd gained a new respect for her. "I appreciate that you genuinely care about Lena. I know she can be difficult at times, but she's always been independent and doesn't like losing that independence."

It was interesting to see how readily Owen was

able to see things from Lena's perspective, yet he'd failed to understand that Laura was in the same boat. Maybe she hadn't always been independent, but now that she'd had a taste of what freedom felt like, she didn't want to let it go.

"I completely understand," Laura said. "I know what it's like to be forced into a situation you can't control."

He took a step back, like he knew she was accusing him. She supposed it wasn't proper to keep pushing his buttons, but Lena's words had gotten under her skin. How could Owen be falling in love with her when he continually failed to recognize how she felt?

But he had comforted her yesterday. And he had respected her wishes when she'd asked him to stop blurring the lines of their relationship.

"Are you falling in love with me?" The words burst out of Laura's mouth before she could even process the thought.

Owen looked even more perplexed. "Why did you just ask me that? Yesterday you said—"

"Lena confronted me just now, I suppose to warn me not to hurt you, but…" Laura shook her head. "I told her to stop meddling in our affairs, but now I can't stop wondering."

She turned her gaze to Owen, his expression no longer readable.

The air between them seemed so still, and as always seemed to be the case when Laura wanted something real from Owen, he was holding back. Even if he was falling in love with her, what good would that do? If he couldn't be open with her, then she wanted no part of a relationship with him.

"I'll just get breakfast started then. You can go sort things out with Lena."

Laura turned to get a small fire going in the cookstove. While it was chilly this morning, the house would soon be too warm for much cooking. It had been unseasonably hot lately, and without the ability to open any windows to catch a breeze, she'd be careful about heating the house too much. There were plenty of baked goods from Mary and other friends who'd dropped food off at the house, knowing Laura had guests and wouldn't have had time to do any shopping.

As she turned to get kindling for the fire, she saw Owen still standing in the same position as when she'd sent him to Lena.

"How many men are outside? I'd like to offer them some refreshment, as well."

"Six." At least Owen had finally found his voice. "But you don't have to trouble yourself. They don't expect anything."

Laura turned back to the stove. "It's no trouble. I wouldn't feel right not taking care of the people protecting me."

"Is that why you're being so helpful to Lena, the girls and me?"

She'd questioned his motivations yesterday, and now he was asking about hers. A fair trade, but as Laura set the water to boil, her hands shook. Honest answers, when they revealed the depths of your heart, weren't easy to give.

Once again, Laura brought her attention back to Owen. "I genuinely like Lena. In many ways, I admire her. The girls…"

Laura took a deep breath. "I've tried very hard not to get attached because it will be difficult to leave them behind and not see them again. But they are impossible not to love."

Of all the heartbreak she'd experience when this was over, saying goodbye to the twins would be the hardest of all. She'd already steeled herself for the eventuality of not having Owen in her life again, but a child didn't understand those things, and she couldn't bring herself to put a wall between them.

But Owen… Laura shook her head, trying to banish the thought from her head. "As for you, I've told you how I feel. But that doesn't mean I'm not going to offer you the same courtesy I would to anyone in my home. I don't know how not to be hospitable."

It didn't surprise her when Owen looked at her like he understood. "You have a good heart. I suppose you can't go against your nature."

His compliment hit her unexpectedly in one of the deep wounds she'd forgotten she carried. James used to taunt her about how she was useless, stupid and so many other things. He'd never looked at her heart. Only Owen saw her heart, and the fact that he could see the good in her that she'd always hoped others would see made their situation seem almost cruel.

"I owe you an answer to your question," he continued. "But the honest answer is the conclusion I think we've already come to. We both feel something, and we'd be liars to deny it. However, this is a tense time, and we're not in our usual situations. Will we feel the same when things go back to normal again? That's the question I wrestle with."

He was right. His words echoed what she'd told him only the day before, and the reasons she'd needed to make things clear between them. Though Lena's questions had temporarily muddied the waters, nothing had changed. Nor would it.

Owen looked at her so tenderly; it reminded her of how he'd held her the day before, only he was across the room. "I'm sorry if Lena's question caused you pain or confusion. I'm glad you told her to mind her own business, and that you told me what she said."

A dark expression flashed across Owen's face, and for a moment, Laura was afraid that he'd be angry with his sister.

Instead, he said, "You have to understand. My late wife and Lena did not get along. Lena saw things in her that I missed, and I think that sometimes, she blames herself for not telling me. Not that I regret my marriage. Without it I wouldn't have the girls, and without them, I would have nothing. So now Lena does her best to make sure I don't get hurt."

As he spoke, Owen's face filled with sorrow. Were the depths of his regrets so much to bear? Though he hadn't told her all the details of his marriage, as Laura thought about the things he had said and was saying now, she could see that his painful past had made him fearful. Just like she felt after what had happened with James. She wanted to move on, but healing was harder than she'd thought.

Then his usual resigned expression returned to his face. "I'll speak with her, though. She shouldn't have said anything. I just hope you don't think less of her for it."

"She loves you," Laura said, trying to sound encouraging. "How can I fault her for that? Don't be too hard on her. I wish I had someone looking out for me like that."

He nodded. "I'm a fortunate man. Thank you for understanding. I should go help her now. I'm sure she's getting impatient."

Laura watched him leave and turned back to finish the breakfast preparations. Though she should have felt more hopeful about their relationship, especially since he'd been more open with his feelings, she realized he hadn't addressed the most important thing: their future.

Lena was sitting in bed, fully dressed, when Owen entered the room. "It took you long enough."

"And you wasted no time."

"I want out of this prison."

Owen couldn't help but chuckle. Were they talking about different things, or was she being deliberately obtuse? With Lena, one never could tell.

But she was eager to be out among people, and he had no problem using that to his advantage.

"I'm happy to help you with that, but first we're going to have a little talk."

Lena groaned. "She told you what I said, didn't she?"

"She did."

He waited, knowing that his silence would make her think, and the longer she thought about it, the more she would convict herself.

"The way you two dance around each other is driving me crazy," Lena said, looking cross.

"You know why I'm doing what I'm doing. Laura is too fragile right now to make decisions about anything romantic."

Lena shifted, groaning as she tried to move her injured leg. "You need to stop deciding for people whether they are or aren't too fragile to handle. Knowing you, you've given her bits and pieces of information, but you haven't laid it all out to try to make her understand. To let her make an educated decision about whether or not you're worth her trouble."

He should have known that Lena wasn't going to automatically take his side. Even though they often put on a unified front around others, Lena wasn't one to hold back when they were alone.

But he was surprised that Lena was defending Laura so strongly. "And what if it's exactly as I fear? And she can't love a rancher with twin girls? These feelings are coming from an abnormal situation. What happens when we get back to my normal life?"

Instead of looking like she understood, Lena laughed. "As I understand things, she let a rooster destroy her parlor, and it lived to tell the tale. Anna speaks of her as though she's the greatest hero who ever lived. Emma has similar stars in her eyes."

After yesterday's conversation with Laura, Owen knew that being a mother to the girls wasn't going to be so much a problem as the rest of it. He had the power to make her deepest longing come true. And, unlike other men who might be interested in marrying her, he wasn't expecting more children. He didn't need a son to carry on the family name. As far as he was concerned, his family was complete as it was.

But was the attraction she felt for him based on the danger or based on something deeper?

And could either of them know the difference?

Lena scooted to the edge of the bed. "If you ask me—"

"I didn't," Owen reminded her.

Lena snorted. "Well, you ought to have. I've known you your whole life, and not one woman has ever looked at you like Laura does. I know you think Sadie loved you in the beginning, but that one always had her eye on the door. Laura just needs you to let her know that her heart is safe."

"What about my heart? How do I know it's safe with her?"

"You're hopeless." Lena sighed as she swung her legs over the side of the bed. "Now are you going to help me out or are you going to sit there dithering about whether or not love is going to hurt you?"

"Fine. Come on. Lean against me, and you can hop on your good leg."

"You're not going to carry me?"

Her false pout made him grin.

"You'd never trust me not to drop you."

"Because you would." Lena used her good leg to stand, then leaned on him. "I'm still not sure you're not going to try something."

Owen couldn't help but grin. "You deserve it for all the meddling you've been doing. If you do any more, I'm going to have every deputy who's available take turns coming in to keep you company. You're pretty enough, and with so few unattached women in Leadville, at least half of them will be interested."

Lena's face reddened, but she didn't say anything. She knew he'd make good on his threat, and she was even more averse to marriage than he was. Not only that, but his sister detested having anyone comment on how pretty she was. Lena was quite attractive, and when they lived in town, he had a number of men ask if they could court her. Lena had always said no.

"Just get me out there," she said. "I want to see for myself the damage that no-good rooster's done. Laura's far nicer than I would have been."

Owen helped Lena out to the parlor, where Laura had already arranged a chair with a footstool for her. She could keep her leg propped up as the doctor had told her, but she'd be far more comfortable than she would have been stuck in bed all day.

"This is a nice room," Lena said. "From the way the girls made it sound, I was expecting everything to be in shambles."

Laura entered the room, carrying a tray. "I've got

tea and some baked goods the ladies brought over. Owen, there's coffee and eggs in the kitchen."

"I'd rather have the coffee if it's all the same to you," Lena said. "And I wouldn't mind some eggs either."

With a smile that Owen was getting used to seeing from Laura as she served others, Laura said, "Of course. You didn't eat the eggs I gave you yesterday, so I assumed that you wouldn't want any. I should have asked. But I do hope you'll try some of the muffins. Emma Jane Jackson made them, and she's becoming quite famous for her baking."

Lena reached for one of the muffins. "Emma Jane Jackson? I didn't know you were acquainted. She would sometimes come with Mary to call on us. She's so refreshing and without pretense."

"Well, if Owen says it's all right for us to have visitors, I can send a message to her and see if she'd like to come by." Then Laura turned in his direction. "I forgot to ask yesterday, but my conversation with Mary reminded me that I would love to spend some time with my good friend Nellie Jeffries."

Owen tried not to flinch at the name. Hers was the last case he'd worked. Though no one seemed to fault him, because he'd gotten distracted, he'd failed to protect Nellie and her children from a wanted criminal. True, no one had been hurt, and the man had been apprehended, but Owen couldn't forget the fact that lives had been in danger because he'd lost his focus for just a moment. It was as if Laura had to poke and prod into all of his wounds, even if she was unaware of it.

"I'll have to discuss that with Will," Owen said, trying not to let the hopeful glances from both women get to him.

Lena wanted him to be open with Laura, to see what the future held for them. But his feelings for Laura were already too much of a distraction. That's why his sister was sitting in a chair at Laura's house with her leg propped up.

If he couldn't keep his focus on making sure Laura and his family remained safe, they wouldn't have a future to talk about.

"That would be wonderful," Laura said, her face lighting up. "We usually have Bible study on Wednesdays, and I'd hate to miss it this week. If Will thinks it safe, I'd be happy to host the ladies."

Laura turned to Lena. "That is if you don't mind. I believe you mentioned that you were once involved in a Bible study when you lived here."

The way his sister looked at Laura gave Owen pause. It was clear she'd found a kindred spirit in Laura, and Laura, too, was fond of Lena. Though Lena had always had friends, she'd acted like she could take them or leave them.

"Yes. I don't regret moving to the ranch at all. But the one thing I miss most dreadfully is being able to share in God's word with other women. Owen will talk about the Bible with me, but I don't think men understand it in the same way."

People often thought Lena's notions were odd. But Laura nodded like she understood. "I think men and women do have different perspectives, but I appreciate both."

Then she looked at Owen like she expected something of him. "Though you've never discussed the Bible with me, so I have no knowledge of any insight you might have."

Lena let out a belly laugh. "Like I said, you would be a fool to let her go."

Clearly his threats of doing some matchmaking of his own no longer worked. But he'd deal with that later.

Instead, he turned to Laura. "I'm surprised to hear you say that, considering we spent hours discussing your fears over how divorcing James would impact your ability to hold your head up high in church. You might recall that I encouraged you to spend time with Pastor Lassiter."

It had been the one time he'd been tempted to cross the line back then. She'd looked so forlorn at the thought of being rejected by God that all Owen had wanted to do was take her into his arms and tell her that it was going to be all right. But he hadn't. He'd done his best to explain that Laura wasn't obligated to remain married to a serial adulterer and murderer. When the desire to kiss her became too strong, he'd brought her to the pastor so she could get answers and he could remove himself from temptation.

His words seemed to shame Laura. "I'd forgotten," she said. "Looking back, I thought I was annoying you with my silliness, which was why you'd had me visit the pastor."

So many miscommunications between them. Yet Owen didn't feel free to explain his actions then, or now.

Gunshots rang out at the front of the house, a reminder of why getting caught up in these emotions was dangerous.

Pulling his gun out of its holster, Owen made his way to the front door.

By the time Owen got to the porch, two of Will's men were headed up the steps. "False alarm," one of them said. "Just a scuffle at a saloon a few blocks over."

The trouble with Leadville was that despite all of the attempts to make it a more civilized place—with the Tabor Opera House, fine hotels and legitimate businesses—saloons and the riffraff that came with the miners and dreams of easy wealth still seemed to dominate the area. Still, it was unusual to have this type of activity at this time of day.

"Which saloon?" Owen asked.

The men looked at each other like they hadn't expected the question, and the one who'd told him it was a false alarm looked a bit shifty. Like something wasn't right with the situation.

Finally, he shrugged. "They all look the same to me."

"I think it was The Thirsty Miner," the other man said.

Now Owen knew something was off. While The Thirsty Miner was notorious for its criminal activity, so much so that most of the lawmen in the area were too afraid to enter, it was on the other side of town. But the man was clearly trying to get him off the line of questioning, counting on the fact that Owen was among those who wouldn't dare enter the place. He was wrong. Owen had been inside many, many times, and it seemed odd that these men were trying to lead him astray.

But Owen nodded pleasantly. "Thank you. Nice work. What were your names again? I'm sure Will would be pleased to hear of your efforts."

Laura might have been distracting him before, but the smug way the two men looked at each other gave Owen confidence that he was finally getting his edge back.

"Jenks, sir, and this is Pitts," said the man who'd given him the inaccurate information about The Thirsty Miner. Not that Owen trusted that these were the men's real names at this point, but it would at least help identify them to Will.

"Well done," Owen said, hoping his words of praise would give these men the false confidence that their plan had worked.

The trouble was, even though Owen knew something was amiss, he couldn't say what it was. There had been gunshots nearby with no explanation. The men were trying to lead his suspicions to The Thirsty Miner, or at the very least, get him to dismiss the gunshots and carry on.

Owen went back into the house, where the women were chatting amiably over coffee that Laura had brought in. Lena had an almost empty plate of eggs on her lap, and it was good to see the color back in her cheeks.

"Is everything all right?" Lena asked.

"No," Owen said. "But I'm not certain what is wrong. Where are the girls?"

Laura smiled. "I just sent them to get a brush and some ribbons so I can do something with their hair. It looks so bad, you'd think Henry had gone and made a nest in there."

Owen walked to the stairs and called up them. "Girls! Come down and say goodbye to me before I go out for the day."

He'd left the front door slightly ajar, and though he hated the idea of potentially using Laura and his family as bait, if Jenks and Pitts were up to something, it would be good for them to think Owen was leaving.

For a moment, his only answer was silence, and Owen's heart fell into the pit of his stomach. But as he started up the stairs, the girls came rushing at him, Henry in tow.

"Do you have to leave?" Emma asked, sadness in her voice. "Laura said that if we got our hair fixed up, we could play a game as a family."

Anna nodded solemnly. "And she said that Henry could join us."

Why did Laura have to be so kind and generous with his daughters? As much as he enjoyed seeing them interact, and how readily the girls had taken to her, Owen couldn't help but fear the way their hearts would be broken when Laura decided that the grand adventure wasn't so adventurous after all.

"Perhaps later. I need to go check something out." He ruffled the heads of each of the girls, noting that Laura's description of their current hairstyles hadn't been far from the truth.

The girls looked sad as they both said, "All right, Papa."

This reaction was one of the biggest reasons he didn't regret moving to the ranch. As a lawman, he'd often had to leave his family for days at a time and spend more time away from home than he liked. Worse, with such a dangerous job, the difference between life and death was a man's focus. He seemed to be losing it more and more. And he couldn't leave these precious children without a father.

He gave them a quick hug and kiss and asked God to keep him safe, to keep the girls safe and, if the Lord was feeling particularly generous, to give him a way after this was all over to sort things out with Laura.

The girls went to the kitchen, presumably for their breakfast, and Owen returned to the parlor. Laura was clearing the coffee things.

"Can you set that down for a moment and sit next to Lena? I'd like to speak with you both, but we need to be quiet about it."

Laura did as he asked, and he was pleased to see that she'd kept her word about following his directions more closely in the future. Hopefully, she'd be willing to do the same today.

Leaning into them, Owen said quietly, "Something isn't right. I don't know what it is, but I don't trust the two men out front, Jenks and Pitts. I want you to keep the girls close. If you could stay in this room or the kitchen, that would be best. No one upstairs or outside until I come back."

Owen looked at Lena. "If I leave you a gun, are you able to use it?"

Lena nodded. "Laura, too. She's the one who covered you when you went to the barn yesterday. I was in too much pain to hold up the gun. Even under pressure, her arm was steady."

The look Lena gave him was meant to shame him. He'd underestimated Laura and her abilities, and she wanted to be sure Owen knew it. He supposed she wanted him to see all the other areas in which he'd underestimated Laura, but there was no time for that now.

"Fine." Owen walked to the closet and pulled out the two shotguns he'd stashed—his and Lena's. He couldn't walk around town carrying one, so he might as well leave it for Laura.

"Do you have a place to hide these closer to you? I'd rather you take people by surprise with the knowledge that you can defend yourselves. If they think you're armed and know how to use a gun, they might come in with more force."

Hopefully, Owen was wrong. He prayed he was wrong. But it never hurt to be extra careful when you didn't have all the information.

"We can put one under the sofa, and the other one can easily be concealed behind the screen. Does that work for you?"

Laura's question seemed innocent enough, but it

stung to see the doubt in her eyes. Like she was trying so hard not to offend and to prove that he could count on her.

He wanted so desperately to reassure her, and yet, with Lena's watchful eyes on him, it seemed like any encouragement he could give Laura would only serve to further Lena's cause.

But would Laura be able to look confidently in the face of any attacker to protect herself and the girls?

Owen would like to think it wouldn't come to that, but so far, he'd been wrong in all of his predictions about how this situation would go.

Looking Laura in the eye, he said, "That sounds fine. Thank you. I have every confidence in you and Lena."

His words didn't change the questions in Laura's eyes, but Lena's self-satisfied snort told him that he could say no more.

"I'll just put these things away and get the girls to come in here, then," Laura said. "Besides, the kitchen is no place for a rooster. The girls will have to learn how to give the room a good scrubbing when all this is over. Lena might be particular about how things are done in her kitchen, but I am not."

As Laura exited the room, Lena nudged him. "You'd be a fool not to go after her."

He shook his head. "And you're a fool to continue this line of discussion when greater things are at stake."

Lena looked slightly put out that her words hadn't hit the intended mark, but Owen wasn't going to let his thoughts get muddled. Not when he needed all of his focus to figure out what was going on.

Chapter Thirteen

It was dark by the time Owen returned to the house. Laura had so many questions, but she was doing her best not to pester him since it annoyed him to have to discuss things with her.

Besides, it seemed like every time they talked, things only became more confusing. Especially when Owen continually alternated between acting like a friend who might want something more and a man terrified of getting burned.

As Laura pulled open the door, she pressed a finger to her lips. "The girls made themselves a pallet on the parlor floor. We told them we were pretending to have a campout. They thought it was great fun. I didn't know if it was safe to put them to bed or not, so this seemed like the easiest way to keep them with us without causing them to be afraid."

Relief filled Owen's face as he entered. Laura secured the door behind him. "Lena is also sleeping. She said the chair and footstool were comfortable enough, so I rearranged her pillows and gave her a blanket."

As if to confirm Laura's words, Lena let out a rather unladylike snore. Even Henry was securely in his basket, and as Laura peered into the room at the sleeping forms, she felt a contentment she'd never dreamed possible. No, that wasn't true. She'd dreamed of such a thing many times. A family of her own, gathered together, content after a happy day. And it had been a happy day, despite the danger they faced.

Laura and Lena had agreed that they would keep the children as unaware of the danger as possible, so they'd turned the situation into a game of pretend, that they were travelers going to a new land through a dangerous territory.

For a while, Laura could also pretend. That this was her family, and the laughter filling her home was not temporary.

But the man shrouded in shadows was a reminder that this would end as soon as they caught James, and Laura would have to once again content herself with being alone.

"Have you eaten? There's a bit of supper left in the kitchen. We made campfire stew in the fireplace, and the girls loved the idea of cooking over an open fire."

Owen gave her a strange look. "Was that Lena's idea?"

Laura shook her head. "No. I'm afraid I got a little carried away with the fun. I didn't think it was a good idea to separate us all long enough for me to prepare supper, and I can't help Lena move much farther than a few feet, so it seemed easier to just cook in here."

Perhaps she had gotten more than a little carried away. But even Lena had admitted that it turned out wonderfully.

"You would have been so proud of the girls," Laura added. "They helped with everything. Even Lena was surprised at how much such young children can do to assist in preparing a meal."

She gestured toward the kitchen. "Let's go sit in there, so we don't wake anyone. Even if you're not hungry, I could use a cup of tea."

Owen peered into the parlor at his sleeping family, then nodded. "I haven't eaten all day, so supper sounds good."

He'd left before she was able to serve him the coffee and eggs she'd prepared, and Laura hadn't thought to make him eat. It wasn't her job, but as much as she tried to keep herself from caring about Owen, she found it nearly impossible.

When they entered the kitchen, Laura turned up the lamps, then busied herself with reheating the stew.

"Thank you for taking such care with the girls," Owen said. "What made you think to do all that?"

Laura turned and smiled at him. "When I was growing up, my parents were so overprotective. I was never able to do anything remotely resembling fun. But we had a wonderful cook who let me spend time with her in the kitchen. Thanks to her, I know how to cook. But she also encouraged me to use my imagination and turned even the most arduous tasks into a game. I always promised myself that if I had children, that's how I would treat them. Since I won't have that opportunity, it seemed…"

Horrified at what she'd just said, Laura took a step back. "I mean, I… That is, I shouldn't have said…"

Owen was staring at her like there was something wrong with her. Which there definitely was, considering she'd just admitted that she'd been using his children to fulfill her long-held desire for children of her own. Which made her seem all the more pathetic, considering Owen would soon be gone, taking the children with him.

"I appreciate that you care for them like your own," Owen said, seeming to be choosing his words with care. Laura braced herself for the *but* that was sure to come.

How could she have gotten so involved in their little game that she'd managed to miss the reality of her situation? And then to admit it to Owen?

She hated the pity on his face, like she was some desperate woman, clinging to fantasies that would never come true.

A frown marred Owen's brow. "After our talk last night, I was afraid that spending time with the twins would cause you undue pain. I don't wish to cause you further difficulty."

"I'll manage," Laura said. "I know we've avoided discussing the future, but may I just request that when this is over, and you bring the family to town… It would mean a great deal to me if you'd at least allow Lena and the girls to call on me."

Her heart seemed to stop as she waited for Owen's response. She hadn't been brave enough to ask him to call on her—she wasn't sure she could take more of his indecision on his feelings.

"Just Lena and the girls?" Owen looked almost wounded that she hadn't mentioned him.

"I've already told you that I was hurt when you didn't call on me before. I won't hold out so much hope again. Not unless you give me a reason to."

Her throat hurt as she said the words, and this seemed to be headed in the direction of another one of their pointless conversations. Laura turned back to the stove to stir the stew so he wouldn't see her expression and be able to read anything into it. Nor did she want to see the pity in his.

"Lena tells me I'm an idiot for not trying to make things work with you. For not talking about the future."

Laura tried not to chuckle. Lena had started to tell Laura something similar, but Laura had shaken her head and pointed out that it wasn't an appropriate topic in front of the children. That had gotten Lena's attention. She might have her opinions about Laura and Owen, but getting the girls' hopes up was going too far, even for her.

"Could you look at me, please? Sit with me?" Owen sounded almost distressed.

Taking the food off the heat, Laura took a moment to gather her thoughts. To ask God that no matter what came out of Owen's mouth next, she would be able to accept it with grace and dignity.

Laura joined him at the table. He'd pulled out the

bench and was sitting facing out, with his back to the table, giving her room to sit next to him.

Owen looked at her like he was afraid of her response. She'd reassure him, but she didn't know that she could do so. Not without knowing where he was going with this conversation.

"I'm sorry I hurt you by not calling on you. I'm sorry that I keep hurting you by not being clear about my feelings and intentions." Owen took her hands and held them in his.

He stroked her hands with the same tenderness he'd used the day before, and Laura could not stop the warmth that filled her. Why did he have to make her feel so good? So safe?

"I want…" Owen shook his head and pursed his lips. Like he was struggling with the words to express his feelings. Laura's heart surged with hope because she knew how he'd been hurt, knew that like her, he was afraid of being hurt again. He hadn't said so, but she had to believe that with as much as Owen had been through, it had made him more afraid to take a leap.

"If we'd met under normal circumstances," he finally said. "I would, without reservation, ask to court you. But the situation we're in, the danger we face, I fear it's clouding our judgment. Would you be willing to put aside these feelings for now? When this is over, can we start again?"

So much of his words sounded like a rejection. Like he didn't want her or couldn't face what was between them. Like what they felt wasn't real. But there was so much tension written across his face, like he feared her response would be negative.

Many of their mistakes in their interactions had been from not having enough information about what the other person was thinking, especially on her part. Laura took a deep breath. No more assuming when it came to Owen.

"What do you mean by start again?"

She looked over at him, trying to find clues written in his eyes.

"I can call on you, and we can see what…feelings…might be there."

His hesitation over the word *feelings* gave her more hope than she'd dare hope before. Was he afraid that she would reject him? That she wouldn't be able to love him, just as the girls' mother hadn't? Or that once she was no longer in forced proximity to the girls, she wouldn't try so hard to care for them?

Laura squeezed his hands. "I'll still be here."

Her answer didn't seem to give him comfort. The lines on his forehead deepened.

She'd thought she'd been wearing her heart on her sleeve, but perhaps she hadn't made her feelings clear. Owen danced around the subject, but maybe it was time someone laid it all out, even at the risk of getting heartbroken.

"I care for you, Owen. I have for quite some time now, which is why your actions have hurt me so much. I've tried to deny it and close my heart off to you. But even now, when you seem so afraid that I won't love you back, it only makes me love you even more."

There. She'd said it. The word they'd both avoided. But it seemed only to make Owen appear more afraid.

If bravery was what this relationship needed to move forward, then Laura could be brave. Even braver, as she dug deep within herself to find the courage to lean over and kiss him.

When Laura kissed Owen, it was as though every wall she'd constructed between them and around her heart came crashing down with that simple touch. And as Owen kissed her back, deepening the kiss and wrapping his arms around her, Laura had never been more sure of the fact that Owen loved her, too.

He might have been afraid to say it or express it with any degree of certainty, but the truth was in his touch.

A man didn't kiss a woman like that without giving her his heart. Not when he seemed to be putting everything he had into that simple kiss. James used to mock her for not knowing how to kiss a man properly, but now she knew that a proper kiss had nothing to do with mechanics, but the emotion rolled up into that simple action.

Owen caressed her, putting his hands on her back, and into her hair as he continued to kiss her. Oh, how she loved this man. Laura couldn't help the sigh of complete joy that escaped her.

Abruptly, Owen pulled away. "What are we doing?" he asked.

Laura stared at him. "Kissing?"

His face was flushed, and she, too, felt a bit warm. Her hair had come down around her face, and she knew she must look a mess. But wasn't that how it was supposed to be?

He stood then walked to the other side of the room. "This is exactly what I was trying to prevent."

"But...we love each other." Suddenly, Laura felt sick. She'd been the only one to say the words. Had she been presumptuous again in assuming he felt the same way?

Owen shook his head. "No. This isn't love. You think you love me because I'm some kind of hero to you. But I am a man, Laura. And I can't let you be this close to me without feeling things that someone assigned to protect you shouldn't be feeling."

Was he trying to tell her this was only lust? Laura's stomach ached as she thought about how she'd responded to him. She only acted that way because of things she'd felt in her heart, not in some baser part of herself. And Owen? Was she so completely blind and stupid to not realize that he was struggling with desire, not admitting his love for her?

The sting of tears on the backs of her eyes made her hate herself even more. She'd offered her heart to Owen, he'd rejected it, and now he was standing here, witnessing her falling apart as he crushed her heart beneath his feet.

"I'm sorry," he said. "I never meant for it to get this far. I have a job to do. This isn't part of it."

She couldn't even be angry at him for kissing her. She'd been the one to initiate the kiss. Owen couldn't be blamed for that. Even though he'd kissed her back with such intensity.

"I understand," Laura said, wiping away her tears. "I shouldn't have been so presumptuous. I'll just get you your supper now."

Sitting here would make her go mad. At least she had something to occupy herself with instead of having to continue looking at the pity on Owen's face.

"Don't bother. I'm not hungry anymore. I'm going to go out for some air."

He didn't look back as he strode to the back door, opened it and let himself outside.

At least everyone else was sleeping and hadn't witnessed the scene. Lena had seemed so hopeful that Laura and Owen would end up together. And for a moment, Laura had almost believed. Perhaps she should have listened all those times when her mother told her not to believe in fairy tales.

Because clearly, there would be no happily-ever-after for Laura and Owen.

Owen stepped out into the yard and sucked in big breaths of air. Why had Laura kissed him like that? And told him she loved him? Did she have any idea what that did to a man?

No, not any man. Him. Owen had had his share of kisses in his lifetime, and none had affected him quite like that. Everything in him had been shaken, and for a moment, he'd thought that he'd encountered the deepest level of happiness that a man could find. Laura in his arms.

What would it be like to have that every day for the rest of his life?

But what would it be like to lose that feeling?

He'd never felt anything like that with Sadie. Not even close. Which made the thought of losing Laura even scarier. But with everything that happened today, and the stakes ever increasing, it seemed only natural that the tension and emotions of the situation would be getting to her.

He'd heard the longing in her voice as she talked about her afternoon with his children. It would be easy for someone to fool herself into thinking she was in love after an enjoyable time with the family. But that was one day. A very good day, from how it sounded. Laura hadn't experienced the hard days. Like the ones when all the twins did was squabble. Or when they were ill.

Would being a mother seem like such a fun adventure then?

That was the trouble with making such a big decision based on such limited information. Laura had seen the good parts of being with his daughters. Not the times when they tried everyone's patience so much, it was hard to know the right thing to do.

And as far as her feelings for him went, how kissable would he be after spending the day mucking stalls? Would she find the day-to-day of ranch life as exciting as the past few days? Because mostly, it wasn't. Which is why it suited him. This running around, hoping his family was safe, doing the best he could to protect them, it got old. His mind wasn't on the job but with his family. Exactly why he'd given up his badge in the first place.

He'd asked her to wait, but she'd jumped right into a fire that neither of them was ready for.

Especially when getting burned meant hurting more people than just Owen or Laura.

Owen paused at the back gate. All the guards were in place as they were supposed to be. A walk to clear his head might do him a world of good. He could talk to Will. About all the dead ends they'd run into this evening, and also about Laura.

Will had fallen in love with Mary while trying to clear his name. A slightly dangerous situation, but no one was actively trying to kill either one of them. Perhaps Will would have some advice on how to handle the feelings that were developing between Owen and Laura. Owen had been hesitant to share all of his feelings with Will, mostly because he'd been afraid that Will would see Owen's emotions as compromising his ability to do his job. Until now, Owen had thought he could manage both, but now, he wasn't so sure.

If only today had given them some good leads. He and Will had spent all day investigating Jenks and Pitts, even going so far as to check out The Thirsty Miner to see if any traps had been laid.

And yet, nothing.

Owen had exhausted all of his contacts, and no one seemed to have any information that he could use.

It was as though James had completely disappeared after their encounter at the ranch.

Will's house was only a couple of blocks away, and when Owen arrived, the place was dark. They must have all turned in for the night. It seemed wrong to disturb his friend's sleep simply because Owen was having an emotional breakdown.

Why couldn't Laura have simply accepted his request to wait until this madness was over?

As Owen turned to go back to the boardinghouse, Will called out to him.

"Did you need something?"

The clouds moved away from the moon, allowing Owen to see his friend sitting on the porch. He should have noticed. One more sign that Owen's skills as a lawman were waning.

"I could use some advice."

Will hopped off the porch and walked over to Owen. "You're doing a fine job. What has you concerned?"

If only it were simply about the case. They'd had a long partnership where they could count on each other to see new angles and puzzle out confusing situations. But they'd never discussed women or relationships. At least not more than in the general sense. Will knew about Sadie, and he knew some of Owen's struggles. But men didn't sit around jawing about their feelings the way Owen and Laura seemed to.

"Laura."

Owen let out a long breath, wishing he had more words to explain that one.

"Are you worried that your feelings for her are getting in the way of catching James?"

He stared at his friend. "How did you know?"

Will shrugged. "A man would have to be blind not to see what's happening between the two of you.

She's been sweet on you for a long time, and it seems like you're finally coming around to feeling the same way."

Then Will looked at him for a moment, like he was examining a piece of evidence. "Or maybe you're just now admitting it to yourself."

"I'm supposed to be protecting her, not thinking foolish things about her."

Will nodded, then started walking in the direction of the boardinghouse. "I've come to believe that the heart knows what it wants, and once it settles on that thing, it's hard to shake. You've protected dozens of women, gotten to know dozens more. But you haven't fallen in love with any of them."

As Owen caught up with his friend, he asked, "Do you think I'm in love with her?"

Stopping abruptly, Will turned to look at him. "Aren't you?"

That wasn't the question. At least not for Owen. "What if she doesn't love me back?"

"What does she say?"

Her declaration earlier this evening would have been the answer Will was looking for; only Owen didn't trust it.

"And what if what she says is only a response to a temporary danger? How do I know it's real?"

Will made a noise like he understood, then motioned for them to continue. "How do any of us know it's real? You ask God for wisdom, and you let His spirit guide you. And then you work it out with the other person. No marriage is about the joyous feeling of being in love all the time. Rather, it's the decision to be committed to loving that person no matter what. Even when you don't feel like it. Feelings are fickle things. But when you're a man of your word, you make a promise to a woman and then you keep it."

Though Will's advice was about marriage and making it work, Owen felt a deep conviction about the promise he'd made to Laura. He'd keep her safe, no matter what. He'd given his word. Owen would be there for Laura, even when it broke his heart to do so.

As they came to the corner where Owen would have turned to go to the back of Laura's boarding-house, Will continued, heading for the front of the house. When they walked past Jim O'Leary's barn, Owen paused.

"That barn door is hanging funny," he said.

Will nodded and put his hand on his gun. "Especially considering O'Leary is mighty particular about things."

"You'll cover me?" Owen asked, not waiting for an answer as he walked toward the barn. He didn't need one, not after working with Will for so long.

As he got to the door, the stench was unmistakable. "There's a body in here."

Owen pushed open the door. Isaac Schultz, one of Will's men, lay sprawled on the ground. A quick nudge with his foot to Isaac's leg told Owen the man had been dead for a while.

"He didn't check in for his shift today," Will said, shaking his head. "Jenks told me that Isaac had fallen ill, asking him to take over. I had no reason to doubt the story."

Then Will grew quiet. "I didn't put it together until now. Jenks told me about Isaac earlier today. Probably around the time of the gunshots. I didn't hear about your suspicions of Jenks until later, and by then, I'd forgotten about Isaac."

Owen closed his eyes and said a prayer for the man who'd been killed. Isaac didn't need to die.

"Let's see if we can find any clues as to why he died." Will said, turning around. "Do you see a lantern anywhere?"

They found a couple of lanterns hanging on nearby posts, and Owen lit them so they'd have light to look around the barn. Within minutes, Owen could see that someone had been living in one of the stalls. The newspapers that lay folded under one of the blankets told Owen all he needed to know.

"This is where James has been hiding," he told Will. "Isaac must have gone into the barn to investigate something, and James shot him to keep him from giving away his location."

Will nodded. "And Jenks must be working with James, so he fed you the story of the gunshots coming from The Thirsty Miner so you wouldn't investigate."

A familiar whinny sounded from one of the other stalls. Daisy. Owen's horse that James had ridden off on. At least he'd be able to return his daughter's horse.

Unfortunately, finding Daisy brought another gruesome discovery: Jim O'Leary's body.

"And now we know why O'Leary didn't notice things were amiss and report it." Will shook his head. "I'm not looking forward to all the funerals."

"So where is James now?" Owen looked around the barn.

"I don't know. Can we make it look like it's been left untouched, so James doesn't know we were here?"

Owen rearranged the blankets and papers. Fortunately, he hadn't needed to move much to get his answers. "It's worth a try. Let's get these lanterns put out and back where we found them."

Will paused at Isaac's body. "I hate to leave him. But if we move him or O'Leary, or do anything out of respect, James will know someone's been here."

"Let's say a prayer for them, and then we'll come back tomorrow. Whether they lie here or at the undertaker's, they're still dead. Isaac was the kind of man who'd do whatever it took to catch the criminals. And O'Leary was a staunch supporter of justice. Let's not let their sacrifice be in vain."

After a short prayer over the bodies, the men made quick work of getting things taken care of. As they exited the barn and made sure they hadn't left any unusual tracks, Owen thought through what they'd seen.

"James probably came straight here after I chased him off, figuring this is where we'd end up. Like he's been waiting for his chance at Laura," Owen told Will.

"So where is he, then?"

Owen didn't need to answer. He took off running for the house. If they were investigating the barn where James had been staying, then James could only be in one place—with Laura.

Chapter Fourteen

Though Owen hadn't lifted his ban on Laura going outside, she headed out back to the well for some more water to finish cleaning the kitchen. She'd seen the guards there earlier, so it should be safe enough to go out for a quick trip.

The air was still, cool, and Laura couldn't help but shiver as the clouds passed over the moon. Owen was out there somewhere, and part of her hoped for a glimpse of him.

Which was incredibly stupid of her, all things considered.

Why could she never leave well enough alone?

"Hello, Laura." James's voice made her jump.

She spun and came face-to-face with her ex-husband.

"What are you doing here?" she asked, looking around for the guards.

"They won't be helping you. A few of my men took their places, and they were good enough to give us some private time tonight. I've been waiting all day for it to get dark enough for me to move around easier."

His voice sounded so even and cultured. Like he hadn't threatened to kill her the last time he saw her.

"What do you want?" Laura kept her voice firm, despite her insides feeling like liquid.

James smiled at her. The kind of evil smile that meant he was going to hurt her. But first, he'd do everything to make her afraid.

Only that wasn't going to work. Laura wasn't that woman anymore.

"I just want my wife back," James said, acting as though he was making the most reasonable request in the world.

She glared at him. "Why? I testified against you. And then I divorced you. Because of me, you went to jail."

Taunting him might not have been the best idea, but it seemed almost ludicrous that James would want her back.

"You know I don't like to lose." James circled her, almost as though she was prey. "I am very upset that you would do so many things to hurt me. And I will make you pay."

She'd known it was about revenge, of course. But hearing his words strengthened her resolve that James was not going to hurt her again. He appeared to be unarmed, but so was she. Could she keep him talking while staying out of his reach long enough for Owen to return?

"I'm sorry," Laura said, knowing that he liked to hear her apologize. Perhaps if she placated him enough, he would let his guard down, and it would make it easier for Owen to catch him.

James smiled. "Of course you are. But what are you sorry for? It seems to me, my dear, that you have made some grave mistakes."

He pulled out a knife, and it shone in the light. She'd wondered why he'd come without a gun, but now she knew. James had never been one to punish her and get it over with. He liked to torment her and make it as long and painful as possible.

Based on what she'd heard of how he'd killed his mistress, it was a momentary outburst of temper. She'd surprised him with the news of her pregnancy, and in a rage, he'd taken a statue and bludgeoned her to death with it. But when James thought he was in control of his emotions, he took his time to exact as much pain as possible.

Right now, he thought he had the upper hand. He thought that he'd somehow outsmarted everyone else here. But he was wrong.

Owen would never leave her unprotected for long.

Even so, all Laura had to do was get inside the house and to the kitchen, where she'd stashed the shotgun Owen had given her inside the broom closet.

At least she'd had the foresight to take that action when he'd left earlier. If she was going to be alone in the kitchen, the least she could do was take the gun and put it within easy reach. Too bad she hadn't thought to take it outside with her. Then, her ordeal would be over.

"You don't look very scared," James said, looking disappointed.

That's what he'd liked. Her fear. And to hear her beg.

It was hard to think like the woman she'd once been. The woman James still thought she was.

"I am." Laura took a deep breath as she stepped back. "I thought…you would never hurt me again."

James smiled, looking so evil it was hard to imagine she'd ever thought him charming. "He promised you that you'd be safe, didn't he?"

Laura nodded. Owen had promised her that. He might not have ever promised her anything else, but he'd at least given her the promise of safety.

"Is that why you kissed him in there? Gratitude for keeping you safe? Or did he demand that as payment?"

Her skin crawled at the thought of James observing what had to have been one of the most humiliating moments of her life. Though he obviously hadn't heard the conversation, it was bad enough that he'd seen.

"Such a shame," James said, chuckling. "You still haven't learned to please a man, have you? I've never seen a man run so fast from a woman's arms. And now he's left you all alone. What a disappointment you must be, unable to give him proper compensation for his work."

James's words disgusted her. He'd gotten it wrong,

but his words still stung. How many times had he berated her because she couldn't make him happy? Though Owen had rejected her, it hadn't been because he hadn't enjoyed her kiss.

Some of the pain she'd been feeling at his leaving eased. Owen wasn't angry with her because of her inadequacies. He was angry because she hadn't listened to him. Not because listening to him meant being controlled the way James had done, but because Owen's warnings were always about her best interests.

She'd seen love and compassion in Owen's eyes. That she hadn't mistaken, even if she'd been wrong about so much more.

James took a step toward her. "I wonder whose arms he'll seek comfort in. It was such a chore for me, always having to find a woman willing to do what you should have done. If only you'd satisfied me and given me a son, we wouldn't be in this terrible mess."

He was a madman, talking the way he did. But the more James talked, the more she realized that all the things she blamed herself for were really about James and his warped view of the world. All Laura had to do was humor him long enough for Owen to return.

With a long sigh, James gave her the look of disappointment Laura knew so well. She used to live in fear of that expression, but now she knew that it had nothing to do with her, only James's unrealistic expectations of her.

"People think I killed Hattie because she was pregnant. Not true. I'd merely asked her to do the right thing, to go into seclusion so we could pretend the baby was yours. No one would have had to know. But that stupid woman thought I loved her. She thought I would leave you to marry her. Why would anyone want to marry a cheap actress who'd been with every man in town?"

James's derision made Laura feel even more sorry for the woman he'd killed. What had James told her and promised her? And how could he have thought that Laura would have been willing to go along with it? Laura shook her head. She'd thought she would have done anything to have had a baby. But would she have been willing to accept his mistress's child as her own?

"You still killed her," Laura said quietly, bringing her thoughts back to the conversation at hand.

James glared at her. "It was self-defense. She flew at me in a rage, so I grabbed the closest thing to defend myself."

Perhaps hitting her once would have been. But James had bludgeoned her repeatedly, making her almost unrecognizable.

"Why didn't you say so in the first place?" Laura tried to sound like she was on his side as she took another step back. Just a few more steps to the porch, and then she could dart inside for the shotgun.

"My lawyer disagreed. But perhaps had my wife been willing to stand by me, he might have had a different opinion."

"You threatened to kill me," Laura said, taking another step back.

James shrugged. "Idle threats. How many times have I threatened to kill you? Are you dead? No."

He sounded like they were talking about the dinner menu or something equally mundane. Just because he hadn't succeeded in killing her didn't mean he hadn't tried.

"You killed people when you got out of prison and said I was next," Laura said, trying to keep her voice calm.

"I wanted to get your attention."

Taking another step back, Laura said, "It worked."

"Are you running away from me?" James came toward her, an ugly grimace on his face. He was enjoying this. Even though Laura was not afraid, because she was finally seeing him for the pathetic man that he truly was, James still thought he had the upper hand.

Let him think that. Because Laura was close to showing him that he wasn't going to win this time.

"I don't want you to hurt me," she said, adopting a more fearful tone. "You said you were going to make me pay. I think I've paid enough."

James snickered. "How many times have I told you not to think? It's unseemly for a woman to think."

It might be unseemly in James's eyes, but Laura had learned just how rewarding it could be to think for herself. And, in the midst of James's taunts, she suddenly understood why Owen had been so frustrated with her. He hadn't been trying to keep her from thinking for herself, or even treating her like the ignorant woman James was. Rather, he'd had a deeper perspective on the situation and had known better than Laura what was necessary. James didn't respect her, period.

Owen had treated her with respect, but she'd been so blinded by her pain over how James had treated her that she'd failed to recognize it.

Lord, please give me the chance to apologize to Owen. He's been trying to reason with me all along, but I've been so stuck in my own frustrations that I failed to see it.

As Laura prayed, she wondered if she'd misinterpreted Owen's reaction to the kiss, as well.

"You're plotting something, aren't you?" James asked, taking another step toward her.

"I'm cold," Laura said, rubbing her arms. "I want to go back inside."

"Are you going to invite me in?" As if he was a guest she welcomed. But there was no way she was going to put Lena and the twins at risk.

"I need to make sure the children are asleep first."

James made a disappointed noise. "Always putting others before me. This is why I have needed to punish you. Don't you know that a husband's needs are the most important?"

"You're not my husband anymore." Laura held on to the handrail as she backed up the stairs.

"What God has joined, man cannot separate," James said solemnly. A fine time for him to recognize God's laws. Especially since he ignored so many others.

In a quick movement, Laura ran for the door and

wrenched it open. James's footfalls were behind her, but she needed only a few seconds, and she would have the rifle in her grasp.

She slammed the door in James's face, knowing it wouldn't stop him for long, but just needed long enough.

Laura grabbed the shotgun and spun around just in time for James to kick the door in. She didn't think but brought it to her shoulder just as Lena had shown her on the ranch. With James so close, she didn't have to aim. All she needed to do was hit him, and he was straight in front of her.

Squeezing the trigger, Laura prayed that this would end her ordeal.

The blast of the shotgun sent Owen running through the house. The precious seconds it had taken him to unlock the door had his heart in his throat. Why had they gone to the front instead of the back? Though both were locked, at least the back was closer to where the shot had come from.

"Stay there," he said to Lena as he passed the parlor. He could see her waking up, but he didn't need her in the middle of whatever mess had happened.

By the time he got to the kitchen, the back door was ajar, with a bit of the jamb damaged from the blast. Laura stood there, holding the shotgun.

"What happened?"

"He got away," Laura said quietly, looking forlorn.

Owen looked her up and down, searching for any sign that she'd been injured. "Did he hurt you?"

"No." She shook her head. "I thought I couldn't miss. But he ran away."

Will reached past him and touched a spot on the door. "You didn't miss. You just didn't kill him."

He turned to Owen. "I can see a small trail of blood. He's not bleeding badly, but it'll slow him down enough for us to gather some men to capture him. He won't go far. If we're right about what we just found in that barn, that's where he's headed. Let's do this right and get some men to back us up."

Owen nodded slowly, unable to take his eyes off Laura. She didn't look scared. Rather, she looked... mad.

"You're sure you're all right?"

She looked down at the shotgun in her hands. "I'm fine. How could I have missed?"

Trying not to chuckle in spite of the situation, Owen patted her arm as he took the shotgun from her. "We practiced with a smaller gun. This one has a kick that, if you don't know what to expect, can knock your aim off. You did good, Laura. You did real good."

The slow nod she gave him told him that she was in shock. It was one thing to know how to shoot a gun, another to face your enemy and pull the trigger.

"Let's get you settled in with Lena." Owen turned to Will. "What do we do about Jenks and Pitts?"

"I'm going to put them in charge of gathering a posse to go after James. They'll pick men loyal to them, leaving the ones we can trust to nab him."

Will kicked at some of the blood in the dirt, then

said loudly, "Looks to me like he's headed in the direction of The Thirsty Miner. I knew that bartender was lying to us. Let's get some men together to go after him. He's been shot, so he'll be slow and harder to hide with all that blood."

Owen turned to see Jenks and Pitts walking into the backyard. Interesting timing, considering. At least Will had noticed them soon enough to give them misleading plans.

Once again, Owen had been too focused on Laura to realize what was going on.

"You say James was shot?" Jenks asked, coming up onto the porch.

"Laura got him, but only nicked him, I think. Don't know for sure. Not enough blood to be a serious injury. He mentioned something to her about The Thirsty Miner, so I think he's headed there. Plus, there's a man there who will fix up gunshot wounds, no questions asked," Will said smoothly.

Laura stilled beside him. She hadn't told them anything about what had happened, and for a moment, Owen wondered if she'd argue. But then Laura nodded.

"Apparently, that's where real women are," she said, her voice sounding dull and unlike her.

The two men looked at each other like they were surprised, but then Jenks smiled. "Then it looks like we've got him."

"Laura's upset by what happened," Will said. "I'd like Owen to stay behind to help her, and I need to advise the sheriff about what's going on. You two are the reason we even knew to investigate The Thirsty Miner, so you'll be up for a commendation, maybe even a promotion. Think you can get together a group of men to round him up?"

Owen tried not to laugh at how eager the two of them looked. How they would let this play out, he didn't know, but in the end, the only thing the two of them would be up for was jail.

"I'll be fine," Laura said. "Owen has a job to do."

He hated how fragile she looked. Worse, he hated that all of this was once again his fault. How could he have left her alone to deal with James?

His stupid emotions. Once more, they'd gotten the best of him, and he'd let his feelings get in the way of protecting Laura. Had Owen been here, he would have gotten James, and this whole nightmare would be behind them.

Owen blew out a breath and put his arm around Laura's shoulders. "Let's get you settled in the other room with Lena. I know the commotion woke her, and she'll want to know what's going on. Besides, you need to tell me the rest of what happened."

Leaving Will to give instructions to Jenks and Pitts, Owen was itching to head back to the barn to get James before he could get away again. But they had to make sure that they'd successfully misled James's men. It all depended on whether or not they thought James was seriously injured enough to need help right away.

He led Laura into the other room, torn between

what Will had directed him to do in comforting her
and wanting to end this.

"What happened?" Lena asked. "The shotgun
woke me up."

The girls murmured in their sleep, but Laura bent
down and gave them a small pat, whispering something he couldn't hear, but it seemed to give the girls
comfort. They cuddled back together, and Owen
couldn't help the tiny twist in his heart.

Yes, he had to end this tonight.

"It seems James paid Laura a little visit," Owen
said. "She managed to scare him off with a shotgun,
but he's still at large."

Lena stared at him. "Why aren't you going after
him?"

"We have a plan," Owen said, feeling the same
distress Lena did. But Owen knew that times like
this, you had to be patient. How many times had he
sat on watch, body aching, waiting for just the right
moment?

Tonight seemed like the most torturous waiting
ever. They knew where James would be. Even better, if he and Will had accidentally moved something
out of place, James would be in too agitated a state
to notice.

Everything would work out perfectly, as long as
Jenks and Pitts took the bait and went to The Thirsty
Miner first.

Lena patted the chair next to her. "Tell me what
happened, Laura. Are you all right? Why didn't you
call for help?"

The look Laura gave Owen made him feel even worse about the situation. Would she tell Lena how he'd let her down? How he'd lost control of himself and allowed his emotions to get the better of him?

"I wanted to clean up a bit, so I went outside to get some water. I could see what I thought were guards out there earlier, so I thought it was safe. Then James walked right up to me."

Owen closed his eyes, willing himself to be patient. She shouldn't have gone out. But if he hadn't left her, she wouldn't have been in such a state that she'd wanted to.

"I know," Laura said, looking at him. "I disobeyed you, and I'm sorry. While James and I were talking, I realized how unfair I've been to you, questioning your orders because it felt like I was being bossed around, and I resented having to give up my new-found freedom. Until now, I hadn't learned to differentiate between being given orders because I was being mistreated, and being given orders because someone cares."

Then she turned to Lena, with an expression on her face that made Owen's heart hurt. "I know I've apologized to you already. But I thought that I was making it up to you, and to Owen, by blindly following his orders. I know now that none of this is about blind trust. Trust is about knowing the person has your best interests at heart and obeying because the other person sees something you can't. I want you to know that I understand now. Which means I can truly be sorry."

Bringing her attention to Owen, Laura continued. "I owe you more apologies than I have words to express. And I know that you have a job to do. I won't waste your time by turning this into another one of our discussions that seem pointless, given the circumstances. However, may I just say that my failure to trust you had nothing to do with you. You're the first person whose actions were about what was best for me long-term, and not what felt good at the moment, or what benefitted you."

The sadness on her face made Owen want to reach out to her, but he knew that wouldn't lead them anywhere good. Not right now. Especially not in front of Lena.

"I give you my trust, wholeheartedly and without reservation," Laura said. "Not because I want to prove to you how much I've learned, but because you've proven to me that you want what's best for me. I'm sorry it took me so long to realize that. If you're willing to forgive me and be patient with me when this is over, could we please start again, as you suggested earlier?"

Her words nearly broke Owen. In a way he'd never been broken before. Laura had humbled herself to a level he hadn't experienced. Perhaps he needed to humble himself, as well.

They'd both made a lot of incorrect assumptions about each other, and Owen had been just as bad a violator as she'd been.

"It would be my honor," Owen said, knowing that this conversation didn't settle anything between them, but he wanted Laura to know that he didn't hold anything against her.

He could hear Will's footfalls in the hallway. "We still face a great deal of danger, and I don't know what's going to happen. But I want this conversation to leave us on good terms, just in case."

Lena groaned. "Nothing's going to happen. So just kiss already and get it over with. You two need to—"

"Work it out on our own," Laura said firmly. "I know you mean well, but if Owen and I are to have a future, it has to be one we make."

Laura gave him a smile. "I'll be praying for your safety. We're on fine terms. I have no regrets."

If only he could say the same. But as Will entered the room, Owen knew there wasn't time for anything else. At least he and Laura weren't in strife. Dealing with the regrets could come later.

"Jenks and Pitts took the bait. I sent Billy Monroe with them to keep an eye out just in case they double back, but they looked too smug to be suspicious. I sent a messenger for a few more men, and we have Bates and MacKinnon guarding the house. Let's get James before the others realize he didn't go to The Thirsty Miner."

Will looked like he had something else to say, but thought better of it. "I put a chair against the back door to keep it closed. We'll have to fix it in the morning."

Then Will held out the shotgun. "I'm hoping you won't have to use this, but I'd like you to have it just in case."

Laura stood and took it from him. "I'll do a better job next time."

Owen couldn't help but smile at her resolve. She was one of the most courageous women he knew, and for the first time, he didn't have fear in his heart about their future.

He followed Will out the door, noticing that Laura locked it behind them. Once again, he was struck by just how much he'd underestimated her. How little credit he'd given her.

Lena was right in that he hadn't given her the chance to decide for herself about whether or not she wanted the normal life he had to offer. And Will had given good advice about a marriage taking work. Sadie had never wanted to make things work but had simply pouted and thrown tantrums when Owen wasn't giving her what she wanted.

Laura had done no such thing. She'd put forth every effort to show him she was willing to meet him halfway, yet he still compared her to a woman she had nothing in common with, other than how they'd met.

It was time to see Laura as the woman she was. To let her tell him what she wanted from their relationship. And to see if she was willing to accept what he had to offer.

But first, they had a murderer to catch.

Chapter Fifteen

They didn't go directly to the barn in case James or his men had lookouts. Perhaps it was overly cautious considering their earlier exploration of the place hadn't seemed to alert any guards, but they weren't going to take any chances on letting James get away this time.

Will stationed some of his men as lookouts at various points between the house and the barn and in the direction of The Thirsty Miner. Now that they knew who the traitors were, they also knew who they could trust.

Everything was quiet at the barn, but Owen noticed that the door was a little more open than it had been when they'd left it. Fresh blood was smeared on the side.

"You think she got his shoulder?" Will asked, pointing to the location of the blood. It was at about the same height as it had been in the house, which was shoulder height for most men.

"Probably. So one arm is useless. That gives us more of an advantage, though a man with a good arm is still dangerous."

Will nodded. "I wish we'd checked for weapons when we were here before."

"Taking them would have given away that someone was here. It'll be fine."

Though Owen sounded confident, he said a quick prayer for protection. He didn't like going into any situation without first bringing it to God, and once again, he was reminded of how little he'd trusted God with Laura. If he trusted his life to God, he needed to trust his heart to him, as well.

As they entered the barn, they heard a moan. "Jenks? That you? I need a doctor."

"Nope," Owen said as he spun and entered the stall where James had been staying. "But we'll be happy to get you one once we get you over to the jail."

Even in the darkness, James looked like he couldn't understand how such a thing had happened. "But Jenks…"

"Is on a wild goose chase to The Thirsty Miner," Will said, holding up a pair of handcuffs. "Now, are we going to do this the easy way or the hard way?"

James shook his head. "I'm not going back to jail. You'll have to kill me first."

For as many times as Owen had thought about ending this man's life, and though he'd come close before, staring at the pathetic creature before him now, Owen knew he wouldn't do it. Nor would Will. Neither of them took pleasure in killing and only used it as a last resort.

Owen took a step forward. "Not going to give you the satisfaction."

James reached behind him and pulled out a pistol. "I'm armed, you have to shoot me."

From the shaky way James held the gun, Owen knew he wasn't capable of using it against them. The injured shoulder, which still seemed to be oozing blood, left his arm lying useless at his side. Based on how James held the gun with his good arm, it wasn't his dominant one, and unlike Owen and Will, James had obviously not been trained to use it.

"Laura has better aim than you with that thing," Owen said, grinning as the other man blanched.

Though Laura hadn't killed James, Owen got a great deal of satisfaction knowing that her shot had incapacitated him enough for them to be able to catch him. The poor guy was probably still wondering where she'd found the backbone.

A quick glance over his shoulder told Owen that Will had his gun trained on the other man. Any sudden movement from James and Will would have him. But Owen hoped it wouldn't come to that. He did a careful analysis of the situation, trying to see the best way to disarm the other man without putting himself in danger. The last thing he needed was for James's lack of control over the gun to cause an accidental discharge that could injure any of them.

There was no need for a reckless action to keep Owen from coming home safely.

Especially when he had another compelling reason to.

"Give me the gun, James. Let's end this like gentlemen and not cause any more harm," Owen said calmly.

James spun the gun in his hand awkwardly, like he was going to toss it in Owen's direction. But then, in an unexpected movement of stability, put it to his head and pulled the trigger.

Owen closed his eyes. Nothing in James's demeanor had made him think that the other man would take his own life, nor had anything in his past indicated that he'd ever been suicidal. But James probably knew that there was no getting out of this situation. He'd have gone back to jail, then to trial on new murder charges, and probably would have ended up with the death penalty. At least with this action, James had been in control of his destiny.

Even if it led to the same outcome.

Will clapped him on the back. "We did what we could. This is probably the best ending we could have hoped for."

For James, yes. And, in some ways, for Laura. She'd never have to fear him again. But somehow Owen thought she might have already won that battle. She hadn't seemed scared of her encounter with James. Rather, she'd seemed empowered.

"Shall we go get Pitts and Jenks?" Will asked, looking around the stall. "I'll have some men come take care of the bodies."

Owen nodded. "Might as well. Though I hate to have to go back to The Thirsty Miner."

"It is definitely not my favorite place," Will said, chuckling. "But at least it will be the last time you have to enter it."

They exited the barn, and Will paused to give the other men instructions. As the clean air washed over him, Owen sucked in several deep breaths.

It was over. Really and truly over. He didn't have to protect Laura anymore. He was free to figure out what it was they had between them.

Will stepped in next to him. "It's amazing how two bodies can stink up a barn, isn't it?"

"Leadville has never smelled so good." Owen looked over at his friend and grinned.

"Go home," Will said. "You did your part. Laura is safe. The rest of us can handle Jenks and Pitts."

Owen stared at him. "But I need to finish the case. Tie up loose ends."

"Is that what you want?"

The look Will gave him wasn't accusatory, but knowing.

"You know my heart hasn't been in it for a long time."

Will nodded. "I knew it before you gave notice. Your priority has always been your family. The older the girls get, the harder it is to pry you away from them. I mean, I love Mary and Rosabelle, but I still love upholding the law. That was never your passion, was it?"

His friend's question surprised him, mostly because Owen had never thought of it that way. He wasn't like Will, who'd become a lawman because he wanted to uphold truth and justice. Owen believed in truth and justice, but it was never why he'd picked up a badge.

"No," he finally said. "I just always wanted to do the right thing. Which, at the time, happened to be becoming a lawman."

Suddenly, he had more clarity about his doubts and fears over being a lawman than he'd had in a long time. He'd thought he'd quit because he wasn't capable of doing the job. But maybe, the real reason was deeper and more important than that.

Still, he had a responsibility to make sure Jenks and Pitts went to jail. "I have to finish what I started."

Will shook his head. "You don't always have to be the hero. Sometimes you can let the other guys have a chance so you can go home and kiss the girl."

Kiss the girl. Owen had done that and messed it up completely. He owed it to both himself and Laura to do it properly this time. To fix what was wrong between them and make it right. Of all the things he'd started, this was the most important thing he needed to finish well.

Will clapped him on the back again. "Go home. That's the right thing for you now."

Owen nodded slowly. "Thanks. I will. Thank you for everything."

Even though Owen knew he and Will would remain friends and a part of each other's lives, he also knew that he was closing the door on this part of his life. Saying goodbye to the badge for the final time. As many times as Will had approached him since he'd retired the first time, and as many times as Owen had said no, this time Owen knew Will wasn't going to ask him again.

He walked back to the house, knowing that the things he had to share with Laura were things he owed her. It wasn't going to be easy, but it was what she'd asked him to do all along.

In the end, it would be her choice to love him or not, but he would give her all the information she needed to make that decision.

She and Lena were sitting on the sofa, shotguns in their laps, when he got back to the house.

"Expecting trouble?" He tried to keep his voice light, but the heaviness in his heart made it difficult.

"Should we be?" Laura asked.

"James is dead. Suicide." He probably shouldn't have blurted it like that, but of all the things they had to discuss, James was the least of them.

Laura nodded slowly like it didn't surprise her. "I think he knew he couldn't win this one. I always imagined him to be so strong, larger than life. In reality, he was only as strong as the people around him were weak. I'm not weak anymore."

The power in Laura's words reminded him of the way she'd spoken to him before he left earlier. She knew who she was, and what she wanted. And what she wanted was Owen.

But as he'd already determined, she needed all the facts first.

He looked at her and smiled. "No, you are not. You are the strongest woman I've ever met, and it's an honor to know you."

Lena made a noise. "Now are you going to kiss? If so, I'd like some help to my room because I do not need to witness that. And if not, I wash my hands of the both of you. Just don't wake the girls. They've managed to sleep through everything else, but I'm not sure how much more ruckus they can take."

Shaking his head slowly, Owen looked over at his sister. "I hope, that at some point in the future, I will be kissing Laura. But first, we need to talk. I need to tell her some things because she needs to know who she's kissing."

He took a deep breath, wondering how to say this next part. He and Lena didn't talk much about their past or their family. But it was time.

"We agreed that certain events would never be spoken of again. But with your permission, I need to tell Laura, because rather than my deciding for her if I am the man for her or not, she needs to have all the information to make an educated decision."

Surprise flashed across Lena's face, but she nodded. "You're telling her everything?"

"Everything." This time, he looked at Laura, hoping she'd understand what a big step this was. She gave him an encouraging look.

"All right," Lena said. "But then you'd better marry her and put us all out of our misery."

"That's up to her." Owen held out his hand to Laura. "Since the girls are in here sleeping, and Lena could use some rest to improve her disposition, why don't we go to the kitchen, where we can have some privacy?"

He shot Lena one of their usual "picking on each other" glances, hoping that her permission meant that things truly were all right with her, and she stuck her tongue out at him. Yes, it was time.

Laura took his hand, and they went into the kitchen. Even though their kiss had been hours ago, it seemed like a whole lifetime had passed since then.

"How about I make us some coffee?" Laura said, going over to the stove.

Though Owen hated letting go of her, he nodded, then sat in one of the chairs.

"I'm sorry for how I reacted to our kiss," Owen said. "The truth is, it was the best kiss of my life, and it scared me. I thought I'd loved Sadie, but she never made me feel even close to that. Losing her nearly killed me, and I was afraid, that once the danger of the situation died down, you'd get bored and leave, too."

"I would never—"

"I know." Owen smiled at her, trying to find the words to explain. "As events unfolded this evening, I realized how unfair I was to you, comparing you to her, when we hadn't talked about any of this at all."

Owen sighed as he sat back in his chair. "I've told you bits and pieces about my family, and about Sadie. But you need to know the whole truth."

His hand shook as he took the coffee from her. She'd had the courage to face her darkest fear tonight, and now it was time to face his.

* * *

Owen looked like a scared little boy, and Laura wanted nothing more than to take him in her arms and tell him it would be all right. But that would be more of a distraction than an aid, so Laura took a seat across the table from him.

"My uncle wasn't really our uncle. We refer to his bride, when in reality, his bride was our mother. We just hated how she lied to him and used him. He married her in good faith, but she still had a husband." Owen looked like he was ashamed of his words, so Laura reached across the table and took his hands.

"Lena and I don't have the same father, as far as we were told. We don't know who our fathers are, and we heard so many stories, we couldn't know the truth even if one of them was true. In the early days, our mother was an actress, though once she had my sister, she became a wealthy man's mistress. She bounced between lovers before and after I was born, and Lena and I were mostly raised by nannies. She kept us in a house she had for us but lived elsewhere. Sometimes she'd visit, but we never lived with her. We were never allowed to call her mother because she wasn't supposed to be old enough to have children our age. So we called her Eliza. I couldn't even tell you if that was her real name."

He looked so lost. Laura squeezed his hands and smiled at him. No wonder he and Lena were so intent on being there for the twins. And why he'd been so heartbroken at Sadie's leaving.

"Then she met Robert Dean. She never told her

lovers about her children, but for some reason, she told him about us. He wasn't able to have children, so he was excited that she had us. Uncle Bob, as we called him, invited us to move in with him on the ranch. He spared no expense making it everything she wanted. She'd only been there a few weeks when she got bored. One day she took off, leaving a note saying that she needed a more exciting life. She said nothing about us, but Uncle Bob told us we'd always have a home with him."

Now Laura understood the fondness with which both Owen and Lena spoke of their uncle. He'd had no obligation to them, but he'd chosen to care for them as his own anyway.

"He raised us, and I loved the idea of following in his footsteps as a rancher. But Lena, she'd known Eliza better than I had, and she missed her. As soon as Lena was of age, she went in search of her."

A dark look crossed Owen's face, and Laura wished she could do more than just hold his hand. She wanted to hold him close to her and tell the little boy who'd lost so much that he never had to fear losing anyone he loved again. At least not in that way.

"When Lena found her, she was no longer the great beauty she once was and too old to attract the kind of men she once had. Lena told her that Uncle Bob would still welcome her, but Eliza didn't want to give up the life she still thought she could have if only she met the right man. Lena stayed with her a few months, and then, one of the wealthy men Eliza had hoped to attract showed interest in Lena. So she made a deal. She'd give him Lena if he gave her good compensation."

Owen looked like he was going to be sick. His cup was empty, so Laura poured him some more. "Drink. You look like you need it."

He gulped the liquid like he hadn't had a drop of anything in days. But the pain in his eyes told Laura his thirst wasn't anything that could be easily quenched.

When he set the empty cup down, he looked at Laura. "She sold her daughter to a man who used her in the cruelest way. I don't know all the details because Lena will not speak of it, nor will she allow anyone to discuss it in her presence. But if you had seen her in those days, you would know that something horrible had happened to her indeed. I became a lawman to find justice for Lena."

All the things Owen had said—and not said— about Lena now suddenly made sense. Laura's heart broke for her dear friend who had suffered so much. "So why do you keep teasing her about finding suitors?"

Owen shrugged. "Lena is a good woman, and she deserves to be happy. Before she left, she was in love with one of Uncle Bob's hands. Tony. He was a good man, and I believe he would have made her happy. But when she came back, she did everything she could to push him away because she didn't believe she was good enough for him anymore. He finally gave up and went away. None of my contacts can find him."

Then he looked in the direction of the parlor, where

Lena and the twins slept. "I push her to find love in the same way she pushes me. We've both been burned, but I believe that, deep down, we both still want it for ourselves, and are afraid to try."

He smiled at her, an expression that melted her heart. "You gave me a reason to believe again."

"I feel the same way," Laura said.

He nodded. "I'm glad. Anyway, I became a lawman, tracked down the monster who'd hurt Lena, and brought him to justice. He was killed in a prison fight not long after he got there. It didn't feel satisfying, especially because, in my hunt for him, I realized how many more men out there were like him. I hated the thought of someone else's sister being preyed upon. I became known for my ability to rescue women from bad situations."

Laura couldn't help but admire how Owen had turned such a horrible event into a way of helping others.

"When I met Sadie, I thought I was in love. That I'd finally found the one thing that had eluded my family—my mother, Uncle Bob, Lena and me. It felt good to protect her, and I was excited to finally have a family that would be whole. I don't know what she thought it would be like being married to me, but she hated being pregnant, hated having a family and hated Lena. I talked to some other men I knew, and they said that a lot of women hated the pressure of being married to a lawman. But also, since she and I met under such strained circumstances, and her life had been chaos up until our marriage, she didn't know how to handle normal."

Owen looked at Laura again, like he was searching for answers in her face. "When I met you, I couldn't help the feelings I felt for you. But I'd learned, over the years, especially after what had happened with Sadie, that a lot of women grow attached to the men who save them from a bad situation. They think they're in love because the man is the first person to be kind to them in a long time. With you, I didn't know if what you felt was love, or if it was something else."

He almost sounded as if he was asking for forgiveness, but as Laura replayed some of their earlier conversations in her head, she understood. "You weren't sure how to tell if what I felt for you was the real thing. But you felt something for me, and were afraid to show it, in case what I felt wasn't love."

As Laura spoke, he nodded. "I couldn't let my heart get broken again. And I was afraid that if I tried to love you, and you decided you didn't want to be with me after all, the girls…"

The weight of his words landed heavy on Laura's shoulders. "You didn't want them to be abandoned again, the way you were."

"Lena and I promised they'd have a different childhood than we had. We couldn't fix what happened to us, but we could make it right for them."

And here he was, trusting her with the information to let her know how important all of this was to him. No, not just trusting her with information, but asking her to be a part of it.

"What happened to Eliza?"

Owen shook his head. "She died alone, in a flop-house, of a disease she'd gotten from one of the men she'd been sponging off. I tried to help her, but in the end, I had to accept that some people don't want our help. Just like with Sadie. Even when I knew she'd run off to be an outlaw's mistress, I still gave her the chance to come home."

"Do you still think I would do that to you?" Laura asked. After all, that had been his fear all along. But surely by now, he'd come to see her character.

"No." His eyes shone with the emotion that had been building inside him all this time. "But I don't know if I will truly make you happy. I think deep down, that's what Lena and I both fear. We've tried to create a semblance of normalcy, but I don't know how to be a proper father or a proper husband. I'm doing the best I can, but even my own mother found something lacking in me."

Laura squeezed her eyes shut to keep herself from crying for the lost boy who sat in front of her, who'd spent his whole life desperate for a mother to love him, and then to have the same situation repeat itself with his wife. How she knew that pain. Of trying to be the perfect daughter to meet the expectations of parents whose desperation for a family had only given them her. Of trying to be good enough for a husband who punished her in every way when she displeased him.

But tonight, as she saw the ways James had tried to control her, and how he'd failed, she'd realized that the person lacking was not her.

Could Owen see that? Could he realize that he was enough, not just for her, or for the girls, but for himself?

"Was there something wrong with the twins that caused their mother to leave?" Laura finally asked, knowing that the biggest key to Owen's heart was those girls.

"Absolutely not," he said, straightening.

Laura nodded. "And was there something lacking in me that made me a terrible wife to James and made me deserve what he did to me?"

"Why would you even still believe that? We all know he's an animal." Owen's face reddened, and he clenched a fist like he wanted to do bodily harm to James.

"Then why do you think it of yourself?"

Owen looked stunned, like she'd slapped him so hard he couldn't move.

Laura got up from her chair and came around to Owen. "The flaw was never in you, and until you believe that, you will never be able to understand how deeply I love you."

When he kissed her, it was with the same abandon as earlier. Only this time, she could feel the love coming out of his heart, completely unchecked. Like he was finally able to give himself fully to her.

"I love you," he whispered, ending the kiss.

Then Owen looked into her eyes and smiled. "But you need to know something else."

Laura smiled back, giving him a quick kiss. "It won't matter, as long as you love me."

"Always." He gave her another quick kiss; then the serious expression returned to his face.

"Toward the end, I thought I couldn't be a lawman anymore because I'd lost my edge and couldn't properly focus on the job. But tonight I realized that it wasn't about that at all."

The expression on his face softened, and Laura couldn't help but think that this was probably the truest glimpse of Owen that she'd ever gotten.

"I became a lawman to avenge Lena. But before that, all I wanted was to be a rancher. Except I was good at being a lawman. Saving women seemed to be a skill I had. Once I became a father, my heart was less and less in it. I hated how I missed the girls when I was on a case. But every time I tried to quit, they needed me on a case only I could do. I kept getting pulled back in."

Owen let out a long sigh. "I messed up on my last case. Nothing that got me in trouble, or left anyone dead, but I thought it meant I'd lost my edge. You probably know of it, since it involved your friend Nellie. I was supposed to be guarding her, and I let a woman I thought was in trouble distract me, and Nellie was nearly killed. It became my excuse for quitting. Now I realize, it was just that. An excuse. I haven't wanted to be a lawman for a long time, but I let myself get sucked in because I thought I was needed. Tonight I realized that someone else will step in to fill my shoes if I let them."

Laura squeezed Owen tight against her and pressed a soft kiss on his cheek. "Nellie did tell me about you, though I don't recall her mentioning your name. For what it's worth, she never blamed you. She thought you were a hero for going above and beyond, risking your own safety to protect her and the children."

He hugged her back, giving her a kiss on top of her head. "That makes me feel better. But it doesn't make me want to be a lawman again. I want to remain a rancher. That's what I love."

Being in Owen's arms made Laura feel safe. And though he wasn't going to be a lawman, that wasn't what she needed to feel secure. "To be honest, I'd find it rather nerve-racking having to wonder if you're all right and knowing that there are people with guns after you. I would be very relieved to be married to a rancher."

Owen grinned. "Married, huh? I don't believe I've asked you."

Pulling away, Laura grinned back. "But you will. And, just so you aren't surprised by how events work out, I'm going to warn you that I plan on saying yes."

When Owen kissed her, Laura was able to delight in him once more. Because somehow, despite all the pain they'd both suffered, together they would find healing.

Epilogue

Laura cast one last look at the boardinghouse as they loaded up the wagon. It was strange to realize that the place that had brought her so much happiness and strength would be hers no more. She and Owen had been married earlier that day in a simple ceremony in the now-empty parlor.

After James died two months ago, she and Owen had decided to create the life they wanted and to do so as quickly as possible. Laura had wanted to marry immediately, but Owen had convinced her that they both needed time to catch their breath and figure out what they really wanted.

But with snow coming, and Owen needing to make preparations for winter on the ranch, they'd run out of time. Not that they'd really needed it. With each day, Laura's certainty about the man who was now her husband had grown.

While Owen went to the other side of the wagon to check a fastening, Laura went to sit on her porch swing one last time. She hoped the new owners would get as much joy out of the boardinghouse as she had.

She closed her eyes to the gentle rocking of the swing. Owen had promised her one at the ranch. A new place for new memories with her new family.

More than that, though, she and Owen had put together a new dream. With the money from the sale of her boardinghouse, they were going to build a new one on the ranch property, similar to what her original boardinghouse had been.

Owen had liked how she'd provided a safe place for women to stay, but he'd quickly noted all the security issues and dangers Laura hadn't thought of. A determined man, like James or one of the other men Owen had dealt with over the years, would have easily been able to harm one of the women. And so he'd drawn up plans for a place on the ranch where women and children in danger could be safe.

More than that, at the new place Laura, Lena and Owen would help the women gain the skills and confidence they needed to navigate the world on their own. No woman should be so lacking in resources that she couldn't escape a bad situation.

"Mama!"

Laura opened her eyes to see Emma and Anna standing in front of her, holding Henry. The girls had decided on their own to call Laura Mama, and she couldn't have imagined a sweeter sound.

"He'll have to stay in his basket for the trip," Laura cautioned. "And keep him away from your aunt. She's still cross that he ruined her best hat."

Anna sighed. "But it was so pretty that Henry thought it would be his wife. And since you and Papa are married, shouldn't we let Henry do the same?"

Laura looked up at Owen, who was coming up the steps. "I believe this is a question for you."

"I don't think so," Owen said, bending to kiss her. "All questions about love and marriage go to you. After all, you taught me everything I know."

"Funny. Because you taught me everything I know."

Laura kissed him back, and the girls giggled. Somewhere in the background, she thought she heard Lena groan, but that only brought a bigger smile to Laura's face. If Lena didn't want them kissing so much, she shouldn't have tried so hard to throw them together. Because Laura fully intended to spend every day for the rest of her life kissing Owen.

* * * * *

Don't miss these other books by Danica Favorite,
also set in Leadville, Colorado:

SHOTGUN MARRIAGE
THE NANNY'S LITTLE MATCHMAKERS
FOR THE SAKE OF THE CHILDREN
AN UNLIKELY MOTHER
MISTLETOE MOMMY

Available now from Love Inspired!

Find more great reads at www.LoveInspired.com

Dear Reader,

I've been playing with the idea for this story for a long time, so when I finally got to write it, I thought it would be super easy. And then a series of crazy things happened, and I had to write this book during one of the most difficult seasons of my life. The verse I chose for this book ended up being fitting, not just because my characters had to learn how to deepen their trust in God, but I did, as well. I learned the hard way that I am stronger than I think I am and can do more than I think I can, but only by the grace of God.

I pray that as you go through your own challenges, you find the same strength in the Lord as I did, and that He'll give you blessings such as a mean rooster. No, wait. You probably don't want a mean rooster. But if you do end up with one, you'll be able to see the blessing in having him. Which might take a while, but when you take the time to seek the Lord's goodness, you'll see it.

I always love hearing from my readers, so feel free to connect with me at the following places:

Website: DanicaFavorite.com
Twitter: Twitter.com/DanicaFavorite
Instagram: Instagram.com/DanicaFavorite
Facebook: Facebook.com/DanicaFavoriteAuthor

May the peace of Christ be with you always,

Danica Favorite

FRONTIER MATCHMAKER BRIDE
Frontier Bachelors • by Regina Scott

When the most influential women in Seattle ask successful matchmaker Beth Wallin to find a wife for Deputy Sheriff Hart McCormick, she can't turn them down...even if the handsome lawman once refused her love. But when she realizes *she's* his best match, will she be able to convince him?

THE AMISH NANNY'S SWEETHEART
Amish Country Brides • by Jan Drexler

After moving in with her sister to act as nanny for her nieces and nephew, Judith Lapp doesn't expect to teach Pennsylvania Dutch to the *Englischer* across the road...or to fall for him. But will he put his past aside to embrace Amish life—and their love?

ACCIDENTAL FAMILY
The Bachelors of Aspen Valley • by Lisa Bingham

After newborn twins are left on his doorstep—along with a note begging him to protect them—Pastor Charles Wanlass marries mail-order bride Willow Granger to keep the babies safe. But can their temporary arrangement blossom into the forever family they both hope for?

HUSBAND BY ARRANGEMENT
by Angel Moore

Pregnant and abandoned by the man who promised to marry her, Rena Livingston must enter a marriage of convenience with Sheriff Scott Braden to save her reputation. The more time they spend together, though, the more she wishes theirs could be a true marriage...

LIHCNM0218

Get 2 Free Books,
Plus 2 Free Gifts—
just for trying the Reader Service!

Love Inspired

YES! Please send me 2 FREE Love Inspired® Romance novels and my 2 FREE mystery gifts (gifts are worth about $10 retail). After receiving them, if I don't wish to receive any more books, I can return the shipping statement marked "cancel." If I don't cancel, I will receive 6 brand-new novels every month and be billed just $5.24 for the regular-print edition or $5.74 each for the larger-print edition in the U.S., or $5.74 each for the regular-print edition or $6.24 each for the larger-print edition in Canada. That's a saving of at least 13% off the cover price. It's quite a bargain! Shipping and handling is just 50¢ per book in the U.S. and 75¢ per book in Canada.* I understand that accepting the 2 free books and gifts places me under no obligation to buy anything. I can always return a shipment and cancel at any time. The free books and gifts are mine to keep no matter what I decide.

Please check one:
- ☐ Love Inspired Romance Regular-Print
   (105/305 IDN GMWU)
- ☐ Love Inspired Romance Larger-Print
   (122/322 IDN GMWU)

Name _____ (PLEASE PRINT)

Address _____ Apt. #

City _____ State/Province _____ Zip/Postal Code

Signature (if under 18, a parent or guardian must sign)

Mail to the **Reader Service**:
IN U.S.A.: P.O. Box 1341, Buffalo, NY 14240-8531
IN CANADA: P.O. Box 603, Fort Erie, Ontario L2A 5X3

Want to try two free books from another line?
Call 1-800-873-8635 today or visit www.ReaderService.com.

*Terms and prices subject to change without notice. Prices do not include applicable taxes. Sales tax applicable in N.Y. Canadian residents will be charged applicable taxes. Offer not valid in Quebec. This offer is limited to one order per household. Books received may not be as shown. Not valid for current subscribers to Love Inspired Romance books. All orders subject to approval. Credit or debit balances in a customer's account(s) may be offset by any other outstanding balance owed by or to the customer. Please allow 4 to 6 weeks for delivery. Offer available while quantities last.

Your Privacy—The Reader Service is committed to protecting your privacy. Our Privacy Policy is available online at www.ReaderService.com or upon request from the Reader Service.

We make a portion of our mailing list available to reputable third parties that offer products we believe may interest you. If you prefer that we not exchange your name with third parties, or if you wish to clarify or modify your communication preferences, please visit us at www.ReaderService.com/consumerschoice or write to us at Reader Service Preference Service, P.O. Box 9062, Buffalo, NY 14240-9062. Include your complete name and address.

LI17R3

If you loved this story from
Love Inspired® Historical
be sure to discover more inspirational
stories to warm your heart from
Love Inspired® and
Love Inspired® Suspense!

Love Inspired stories show that
faith, forgiveness and hope have the power
to lift spirits and change lives—always.

Look for six new romances every month
from **Love Inspired®** and
Love Inspired® Suspense!

"Beth, stay away from the docks. There are some rough
sorts down there."

The two workers hadn't seemed all that rough to her.
"You forget. I have five brothers."

"Your brothers are gentlemen. Some of those workers
aren't."

She really shouldn't take Hart's statements as anything
more than his duty as a lawman. "Very well. I'll be careful."

His gaze moved to the wharves, as if he saw a gang of
marauding pirates rather than busy longshoremen. "Good. I
wouldn't want anything to happen to you."

Beth stared at him.

"I'd hate to have to explain to your brothers," he added.

Well! She was about to tell him exactly what she thought
of the idea when she noticed a light in his eyes. Was that a
twinkle in the gray?

Beth tossed her head. "Oh, they'll take your side. You

know they will. They always say I have more enthusiasm than sense."

He shrugged. "I know a few women who match that description."

Beth grinned. "But none as pretty as me."

"That's the truth." His gaze warmed, and she caught her breath. Hart McCormick, flirting with her? It couldn't be!

Fingers fumbling, she untied the horses and hurried for the bench. "I should go. Lots to do before two. See you at the Emporium."

He followed her around. Before she knew what he was about, he'd placed his hands on her waist. For one moment, she stood in his embrace. Her stomach fluttered.

He lifted her easily onto the bench and stepped back, face impassive as if he hadn't been affected in the slightest. "Until two, Miss Wallin."

Her heart didn't slow until she'd rounded the corner.

Silly! Why did she keep reacting that way? He wasn't interested in her. He'd told her so himself.

She was not about to offer him her heart. There was no reason to behave like a giddy schoolgirl on her first infatuation.

Even if he had been her schoolgirl infatuation.

She was a woman now, with opportunities, plans, dreams for a future. And she wasn't about to allow herself to take a chance on love again, especially not with Hart McCormick.

For now, the important thing was to find the perfect woman for him, and she knew just where to look.

Don't miss
FRONTIER MATCHMAKER BRIDE by Regina Scott,
available March 2018 wherever
Love Inspired® Historical books and ebooks are sold.

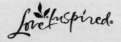

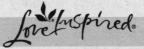
*Fresh off heartbreak, will Helen Zook find peace in
Bowmans Corner...and love again with her new boss?*

Read on for a sneak preview of
AN UNEXPECTED AMISH ROMANCE
by **Patricia Davids**,
available March 2018 from Love Inspired!

Mark Bowman lifted his straw hat off his face and sat
up with a disgruntled sigh. Trying to sleep on a bus was
hard enough, but the sound of muffled weeping coming
from the seat behind him was making it impossible.
He turned to look over his shoulder. The culprit was
an Amish woman with her face buried in a large white
handkerchief. She was alone.

"*Frauline*, are you all right?"

She glanced up and then turned her face to the window.
"I'm fine."

It was dark outside. There was nothing to see except
the occasional lights from the farms they passed. She
dabbed her eyes and sniffled. She was a lovely woman.
Her pale blond hair was tucked neatly beneath a gauzy,
heart-shaped white *kapp*. He didn't recognize the style
and wondered where she was from. "You don't sound
fine."

"Maybe not yet, but I will be."

The defiance in her tone took him by surprise and
reminded him of his six-year-old sister when she didn't
get her way. Experience had taught him the best way to

stop his sister's tears was to distract her. "I don't care much for bus rides. Makes me queasy in the stomach. How about you?"

"It doesn't bother me."

"Where are you headed?"

"To visit family." The woman's clipped reply said she wasn't interested in talking about it. He should have let it go at that, but he didn't.

"Then someone in your family must be ill. Or perhaps you are on your way to a funeral."

She frowned at him. "Why do you say that?"

"It's a reasonable assumption. You'd hardly be crying if you were on your way to a wedding."

Tears welled up in her eyes and spilled down her cheeks. With a strangled cry, she scrambled out of her seat and moved to one at the rear of the bus, effectively ending their conversation.

Confused, he stared at her. Somehow he'd made things worse, and he had no idea what he'd said that upset her so. He shook his head in bewilderment.

Don't miss
AN UNEXPECTED AMISH ROMANCE
by Patricia Davids,
available March 2018 wherever
Love Inspired® books and ebooks are sold.

www.LoveInspired.com